Talking to Tubby

Book Three of The Drugstore Series

ALSO BY SD SHELTON

Me, the Crazy Woman, and Breast Cancer

The Drugstore

The Life of Old Pete

Talking to Tubby

Book Three of The Drugstore Series

A NOVEL

by

SD Shelton

ENLIGHTEN
PRESS

ENLIGHTEN PRESS

A DIVISION OF ENLIGHTEN COMMUNICATIONS, INC.

Enlighten Press
A Division of Enlighten Communications, Inc.
Norman, Oklahoma

Talking to Tubby
The Drugstore Series: Book Three
All Rights Reserved
Copyright © 2018 by SD Shelton

First Enlighten Press trade paperback edition April 2018

Cover Design by Elizabeth B. Wren

Manufactured in the United States of America

10 9 8 7 6 5 4 3 2 1

Paperback ISBN 978-0-9825085-7-2
EBook ISBN 978-0-9825085-8-9
Library of Congress Control Number: 2018903312

For more information about special discounts for bulk purchases, please contact Enlighten Press at enlightenpress@cox.net

For Lynette LaMascus,

who gifted me Maxwell,

the best animal I have ever known.

"Some people talk to animals.

Not many listen though.

That's the problem."

— A.A. Milne creator of Winnie-the-Pooh

Chapter One

Tubby Anderson turned his head to the left and smelled the hay upon which he laid. It smelled different from the normal hay.

"Maybe this here is Bermuda steada Alfalfa," he turned to the large swollen pig lying next to him.

"You okay Miss Minnie?" he asked her, before she grunted her reply.

Tubby had raised Miss Minnie since she was born. She was so small that the other piglets in the litter wouldn't allow her to suckle. Tubby was infuriated that Minnie's siblings were so selfish.

"I'll shows ya," he huffed at them, then picked up the tiny, pink and squealing animal. He stuffed her into the pocket on the bib of his overalls and took her inside the family's mobile home.

"I need me a bottle Ma," he told his mother who was in the kitchen frying some eggs.

"Why?" she questioned her oversized son.

"The piglets won't let this un here feed," he said while pulling out the now quiet piglet.

"Tubby, you're gonna have to learn that things are the way they are for a reason. Only the strong survive and if this one can't feed, it's not supposed to," she rationalized.

"No Momma, that ain't right. This here's a fine pig en I'm aim ta take care of it. She's gonna be big en strong, just like me." He nuzzled the tiny snout looking up at him.

Tubby's mom shook her head and sighed. "Don't know if I still got one small enough for her," she said, sizing up Tubby's newest project. "See if this one will work." She handed Tubby what looked like a doll bottle.

Tubby took the bottle and returned the pig to his pocket. He got a small and slightly rusted sauce pan from the cabinet next to the stove. He got some of the morning's milk that his father, C.J., short for Clarence Junior, had gotten from their lone milk cow, Penelope. Tubby poured it into the pan and turned the burner on low to warm.

While waiting, he sat down at the red Formica kitchen table. The table had been one of a very few things they were able to save after a big tornado had come through Konawa, Oklahoma, fourteen years earlier in 1962. It destroyed a large part of the town and the surrounding area, including their little farm house, which sat a few miles southeast of the small community.

Tubby's parents didn't have any insurance and couldn't rebuild, so his father had put down everything they had on the used trailer house and made monthly payments on the balance.

Tubby remembered the storm, although he was only around seven when it happened. His Pa had seen it coming over the ridge and hollered at his momma and him to get to the cellar. Tubby was in the front yard playing with his dog Oscar. His momma had been inside making supper. Tubby grabbed Oscar by his collar and forced him around the side of the house, wondering why they were going to the cellar in February.

"Cellar time's in spring, not winter," he thought.

"Hurry up Son!" his father continued yelling. "Leave that dog and come on!"

Tubby ignored the order. There was no way he was going to leave his best friend in the world. No way.

Tubby tugged at the dog and ran as fast as he could, but the wind was so strong it kept blowing them back, making the short trip very difficult. When he came around the corner of the house, he saw his momma bounding down the stairs of the cellar while his dad struggled to hold the old plywood door open against the wind.

"Come on Son!" Tubby heard panic rise in his father's voice. It was something he hadn't ever heard before, and he knew something terrible was happening. It was then that Tubby looked over the ridge and saw the black, and very wide funnel approaching. He tried to run faster but the wind was like a brick wall, forcing Tubby to use every ounce of strength he had, just to take a step.

Tubby was only a couple of feet from the door when he felt his father lift him from the ground and throw him down the stairs. Tubby kept hold of Oscar for all he was worth, and both he, and the dog, tumbled to the floor. The next thing he knew, he was laying on the cold concrete with Oscar shivering beside him.

His father yelled to his momma to help him secure the door. While C.J. struggled with all his might to hold the door closed, Myrtle Anderson grabbed the end of the long tractor chain that was attached to the door handle. She latched the end to another link, forming a loop. Then she slid it around one of the pipes of the well pump that was housed inside the cellar.

C.J. continued to hold the chain, as the door lifted in waves like it was gasping for breath. It banged against its frame again and again.

A horrible roar, similar to a freight train barreling down upon them, swept overhead. The earth around the dugout shook as if they were underneath a buffalo stampede. It felt to Tubby like a giant vacuum sweeper had been stuck down the ventilation shaft, removing all the air in the small room. He struggled to get a breath before pulling his shaking arm up to push the wind-blown hair from his eyes. That is when he noticed the blood on his arm.

He tugged at his mother's apron and pointed to his arm. She gasped. It was coated in blood, so she could not see the source. She untied her apron and pulled it over her head. She began frantically wiping Tubby's arm while searching for the location of the injury. Her apron was soaked by the time she located the wound, about an inch below his elbow. The gash was only about three inches long, but it was very deep. She tied the strings of the apron around his bicep and tightened them so much that Tubby yelped. She took the rest of the apron and wrapped it around Tubby's forearm, trying to keep the blood at bay.

Tubby was perplexed. He saw the blood, and he saw the wound from which it came, but he felt no pain.

"Why?" he wondered. *"This should really hurt."*

Myrtle, a large woman herself, also tried to catch her breath, her large bosom heaving laboriously. She wanted to put on a brave face for her son, but she knew the cut was going to require stitches. She also knew the emergency room bill was going to be a hardship for their family.

"You do what ya gotta do," she tightened her lips into a thin and stark line.

"How are you baby?" she asked the boy.

"I'm okay Momma," Tubby replied. "It don't hurt at all," he shrugged.

"That's the adrenaline. It happens when you get scared and it protects ya, but as soon as it wears off – well, let's not think about it," she said, pulling the boy in close to her.

"You okay Daddy?" she asked, turning to her husband.

C.J. still had a tight clutch on the chain, as if his reinforcement was any match for the beast they were encountering. He turned to look at Myrtle, who saw he was white as a ghost.

"It's February." The look of confusion on his face told the strange story. "How we gettin' a tornado in February?"

Myrtle sighed, shaking her head. "Heaven only knows. Seems like the weather's gettin' stranger all the time."

C.J. nodded his head in agreement. "Wudn't any rain or any hail with it," he furrowed his brow. "Wudn't no stillness or no green." He contemplated the missing components of the unique storm.

"You're right. Rain, followed by hail, followed by nothin'," she recounted the old-timers formula for a tornado. "Wasn't any a that. Maybe there wasn't no green 'cause it's February?" she guessed.

Anyone who'd been around tornado alley for any length of time knew how to spot the signs of the deadly storms. First, it was most likely spring time. Second, there would be a thunderstorm with rain, sometimes a gully-washer. Third, there would be a downpour of hail, before everything would get deadly silent. The atmosphere would change into a green and charged haze, which would be followed by complete stillness, and sometimes, even a little sunshine.

Just as quickly as the stillness came, the air would fill with a smell of sweet earth and ancient minerals. That's when on-lookers knew to search the southwest sky. Invariably, they would spot the massive black wall cloud, with a lowering funnel, which sagged like a belly on a fat man.

A shiver went up C.J.'s spine with the realization that none of the signs had occurred. He recalled that the animals had been strangely restless that day – pacing a little and calling to one another, but it never occurred to him that there was a tornado on the horizon – a cold front maybe, but not a tornado. This storm had come out of the blue, and if he hadn't been coming in from the barn, and felt the strange gust at that exact moment, his family might have all been killed. He felt his knees try to give way. This had been as shocking of a storm as he had witnessed in all his years in Oklahoma. He hoped it would be his last.

The roar died down, and the air had also returned to the cellar, allowing everyone to breathe without restraint. Oscar whimpered at Tubby's feet. Tubby leaned over and clutched the dog's head with his good arm.

"It's okay Oscar," Tubby soothed, while rubbing him back and forth. "We're all okay now. Don't ya worry, we're gonna be fine," he assured the black mutt.

Oscar wasn't buying it however. He looked at Tubby's arm and whined again, before he licked the boy's free hand. Tubby continued to pet the dog while nervously looking to his father.

"What about the rest of 'em Pa?" he tilted his head toward the barn.

"Shhh," C.J. answered, before cocking his head to hear what else was happening outside.

Besides a small amount of wind, everything was quiet. C.J. took the chain from around the pipe and began to lift the old cellar door. Dusk had set in, darkening the landscape. It took him several minutes to understand what he was seeing.

At first, he thought he was disoriented – that maybe he had hit his own head on the way down into the shelter. He shook it to clear the cobwebs, but the scene before him remained the same. Where he would have normally seen their back porch, he saw nothing but a pile of debris. There was also a small tin shed lying against the debris. It was what used to be a storage shed for farm tools and implements. Most of the small outbuilding was intact, but some parts were missing. C.J. surmised that it must have been what had hit Tubby and sliced his arm. He knew he had seen something fly by as he grabbed his son just as the boy was going airborne. He hadn't meant to throw him so forcefully, but it was either that, or let the storm take him.

When the realization that their house was gone finally set in, C.J. turned the opposite direction to see if the barn had been taken too.

What he saw caused him to sigh deeply, tears welling in his eyes. The barn was in perfect order. C.J. couldn't wrap his mind around it. It was true that the barn was a good fifty yards from the house, but still, how could it possibly still be standing? It didn't make sense to him.

Myrtle tugged on his shirt and he turned to look down the stairs at his wife and son, their faces questioning him as to what he had seen.

"It's gone Momma," the words choked him a little.

Myrtle gasped and put her hand over her mouth.

"The barn's still here though," he tried to erase a little of the heartbreak on his wife's face. "That means the animals are all okay too," he assured Tubby.

Myrtle's hand didn't leave her mouth until she used it to push C.J. aside so she could see for herself. When she did, the gasp, as well as the hand, returned. She stood shaking her head back and forth as if doing so could change what she was seeing. The scene before her was too much for her to comprehend.

"How is this possible?" she questioned the heavens. "I was just making dinner in there," she pointed to what remained of her once warm and cozy house – the place where she had birthed her son and a stillborn daughter.

"It's all gone." Myrtle hit her knees and sobbed.

"Now there Momma." C.J. knelt beside her, rubbing her back. "We still have each other, and that is all that matters."

Myrtle looked up at him and nodded. She sucked in her breath and stood up.

"Yes. That's right." She set her chin. "We are still here and that is all that matters. Come on Tubby." She turned and motioned to her son to come up the stairs. "We got to take you to the hospital in Maiden and get your arm looked at."

Tubby hesitantly climbed the stairs and peeked out at the devastation. It was a moment he would never forget, as it taught him one of the most powerful lessons of his life. You can't take anything for granted, and you have to make sure everyone you love knows it because everything can change in an instant.

Chapter Two

Tubby got up from the table to check the milk for his piglet. Because the old stove was about to give up its life, the liquid was only slightly warm. He sat back down at the table, and remembered the trip to Maiden to stitch up his arm.

His momma had grabbed an old shirt from behind the pickup's bench seat and wrapped it around Tubby's arm, after she removed her soaked apron.

"Just hold it up Tubby, and try and keep the blood inside ya," she told him. The short drive seemed to take forever. Tubby could tell that his mother was worried. Every so often, she sucked in a big breath, and let it go with a little "whoo" sound.

"You okay Momma?" Tubby couldn't hide his own worry.

"I'm okay sweetie," she smiled. "Just tryin' to get my nerves to calm down. That was a scary thing that happened back there." Myrtle went silent for a moment, and her face turned sad. "Don't know what we're gonna' do for a roof over our heads."

Tubby sunk a little lower in the seat, more nervous now than he had been. It became all he could think about, until they pulled into the emergency room entrance of Valley Brook Hospital.

Myrtle helped her son out of the truck, and led him into the emergency room. She saw a couple of other residents of Konawa in the waiting room.

"Ya'll okay?" she asked the assembly.

Marjorie McCrory, who owned a small diner downtown, nodded. "We all just got some bumps and bruises."

Marjorie zeroed in on Tubby. "He gonna be okay?"

"He got hit with some flyin' debris. I think he just needs some stitches."

The group nodded.

Myrtle turned to the receptionist, and told her that they needed to see the doctor. The clerk looked over her glasses at Tubby.

"Is he still bleeding?"

"Yeah, but not as bad as he was." Myrtle took Tubby's hand and held onto it.

The clerk nodded. "Take a seat and we will get to you as soon as we can. Won't be too long though," she reassured the worried mother.

Myrtle wrung her hands and sighed. "Sit there," she pointed to a row of empty seats against the far wall.

"Your boy get hurt in the tornado?"

Myrtle turned to see Festus Marney, a widower who lived a little northwest of town.

Myrtle nodded while putting Tubby into a chair. "Did you get damage?"

"No, not my place, but most of Konawa did, especially Main Street," he shook his head. "I was in the diner when it hit. Got cut here by some glass. Nothin' serious." He showed Myrtle his bicep.

"You say most of Main Street was hit? How bad was it?" Myrtle looked concerned.

"Purty bad," Festus exhaled loudly. "Church steeple and roof is gone at First Baptist, and most of the stores are in tatters. Some are ruined." He bit into his lower lip.

"Our house is go..." before Myrtle could finish her sentence, the reality of losing her home hit her. She sunk into a chair next to her son, and buried her head, sobs escaping from her heart-broken chest.

Festus got up from his seat and walked to Myrtle. He sat down next to her.

"Oh my, Mrs. Anderson, I'm so, so sorry."

Then he frantically began looking around.

"Where's C.J.?" he asked, fearing the worst.

"He's okay," Myrtle sniffed. "He's back at the farm, trying to salvage anything he can."

She pulled a tissue from her purse and wiped her eyes before blowing her nose and pulling herself together.

"It's okay; we're all okay; the barn's okay, and the animals are okay. It could have been worse," she reminded herself.

"Where are you folks gonna stay tonight?" Festus asked.

"Don't rightly know," Myrtle answered. "The barn, maybe." It was then that she began devising a plan to go to the neighbors and borrow a couple of blankets.

"Oh no," Festus interrupted her thoughts, "you aren't staying in your barn. I got that big ole farm house and just me livin' in it. Got more than plenty of room for ya'll. This un here can even have his own room," he smiled at Tubby, who shyly returned the smile.

Myrtle sat for a moment, trying to give rise to an argument, but she had none. They were going to need a place to stay. There was no way around it.

"You are too kind Mr. Marney. I 'preciate it and I know C.J. will too. Thank you," a little sob escaped again.

"Marney!" a large nurse entered the waiting room and looked around.

"No, no," the man stood up and faced the nurse. "Take this here boy first; he's hurt worse than I am," he pointed to Tubby.

"Thank you so much, Mr. Marney," Myrtle said again, turning to the man.

"It's Festus, and don't you worry about it none. It's the least I can do. As soon as you get your youngin taken care of, get C.J. and come on over. I'll have some dinner, and your rooms ready for ya," he smiled again, as Myrtle agreed.

The shirt around Tubby's arm was as soaked as the apron had been. Worse, the adrenaline had worn off, and the injury was more painful than anything Tubby had ever experienced.

The nurse led Tubby and his mother back into a small curtain partitioned area of the emergency room. They sat the boy on a gurney. The nurse explained that they would need to clean his wound before the doctor looked at him.

As soon as the alcohol soaked cotton ball hit the cut, Tubby let out a little whine. He winced but tried not to cry because he didn't want anyone to think he was a sissy. It took everything he had to hold back the tears. His mother saw his anguish and tried to soothe him.

"Look how brave ya are, Tubby. I'm so proud of ya."

Tubby half-heartedly smiled at her. "I'm okay Momma," he sniffed.

"Yep, it's a pretty deep gash," the nurse told Myrtle when she had finished. "Doc will be here in a minute." She closed the curtain and left them alone.

Myrtle talked to Tubby about fishing to help take his mind off the pain.

"Pa said there are gonna be some big catfish in the pond this fall. If you'll go catch 'em, I'll fry 'em up with some hushpuppies – just like you like 'em."

Tubby nodded in agreement, when the curtain opened again. A tall lean man with a white coat and stethoscope around his neck came to the edge of the gurney.

"Tornado got ya?"

Tubby nodded.

"Let's have a look here." The man lifted Tubby's arm and examined the wound. "Gonna need some stitches youngin. You are very lucky though," he clicked his tongue. "If you'd been hit in the head, there's no telling how much damage would have been done."

Myrtle gasped at the thought.

"We'll get him fixed right up though," the man reassured Tubby's mother.

The doctor left and a much younger man entered. "Hi, I'm Dr. Pinley. I'm a resident intern here and I'm going to be taking care of your son," he looked to Myrtle before having Tubby lay down on the gurney.

"We're just gonna cover your face here so that you can relax," the young doctor told Tubby, before he placed a sterile paper like blanket over the boy's head.

It was strange to Tubby that he could not see anything around him. He felt his mother grab the hand of his unharmed arm before he felt a sharp stabbing pain in the injured one. He jumped, while at the same time yelling. Salty tears stung his eyes.

"It hurts Momma," he cried.

"It's okay Tubby," his mother gently stroked his hand. "It's okay my sweet boy."

Tubby could tell his mother was crying too, and this made him want to be brave more than anything. Tubby couldn't stand to see his mother cry. It was as if someone took a jagged knife and cut through his heart, when she did.

He felt the stabbing pain again and, although he had promised himself he wouldn't, he let out another yell, which was accompanied by the jumping and tears.

"Momma please make em stop," he begged.

Myrtle squeezed his hand, trying to comfort the boy. "Hold on baby, he's almost through."

But he wasn't. The doctor continued sewing the arm and Tubby continued to wince and cry out – the blue paper sheet floating off his face each time he jumped.

Finally, when he thought he could stand it no more, the doctor pronounced it was over.

"Six stiches," he smiled with pride, as he removed the sheet from Tubby's face. He then showed the boy the sewn and intact wound.

Tubby was not nearly as pleased as the young caregiver seemed to be. He continued to cry while trying to ignore the pain.

It wasn't long before the senior doctor returned to examine the work of his charge.

He looked over the wound then at Tubby. "This will be a great story to tell your friends," he smiled, "and it didn't hurt too much now did it?"

"Oh yes it did!" Tubby hollered. "It hurt worse than anything I've ever had hurt!" He stuck out his lip to pout.

The doctor turned to the intern. "You deadened the area didn't you?"

The intern's face turned ashen. He looked from Myrtle, to Tubby, and back to his mentor, before taking a deep breath.

"Ummm," he stalled, not wanting to admit his error. He looked at the floor before finally confessing. "I forgot."

At the same time, both Myrtle's and the doctor's eyes bulged. Tubby looked back and forth between them, not understanding the silent conversation. The attending physician turned to Tubby's mother.

"I am so very sorry," he apologized. "I never in my wildest dreams thought this – this," he searched for the right insult as he pointed to the younger physician, "imbecile," he finally managed, "would forget to give your son an anesthetic." The senior doctor put his hands on his hips and glared at the intern.

Myrtle realizing the pain that Tubby must have endured, rushed to hug the boy. "I'm so, so, sorry Tubby!" she shook her head glaring at both the men. "Let's go!" she spat as she helped her traumatized son off the gurney.

"Of course there will be no charge for this," the seasoned doctor called after her. Myrtle turned back to glare again, biting her tongue to keep from causing the biggest scene she had ever caused.

As she helped Tubby walk to the pickup, she regained her composure in order to spare Tubby even more upset.

"Ice cream," she announced, as soon as she loaded him and then herself into the truck. She looked at her boy to see if her idea might turn the evening around a little.

Tubby nodded, a small smile crept across his face. "Chocolate," he said. "Double dip."

Myrtle smiled in return, and headed toward the small ice cream parlor, a few blocks from the hospital. It wasn't a time to be concerned about spoiling the boy's dinner.

"If it makes him feel even a little better, I'll buy him a gallon," she thought.

Tubby had been terrified of storms ever since the day the tornado hit. In fact, if the sky clouded over in the least, he would get Oscar and go sit next to the cellar, eyes fixed to the sky until C.J. or Myrtle came outside to tell him not to be afraid. C.J. even taught him the types of clouds so that he would know which ones he could ignore. It would take many years though, before Tubby would feel comfortable enough to let a thunderstorm pass without barricading himself near or inside the shelter.

Chapter Three

T ubby lay beside Minnie, rubbing her big belly and talking to her soothingly. That first bottle, when he was nine years old, had turned into many, and he had been right. Because of his love and care, thirteen years had passed and Minnie had grown up to be big and strong. She had even produced several litters of piglets throughout her lifetime, before Tubby had put his foot down about his father breeding her.

"You can't do it to anymore Pa," he told C.J. several years back. "She can't take losin' her babies. It makes 'er too sad."

C.J. tried to reason with his son, and explained that breeding was her purpose.

"If we're gonna continue feedin' 'er, she has to earn 'er keep," he flatly stated.

However, Tubby was having none of that. He forcefully told C.J. that Minnie had already earned her keep, and she was not just a farm animal, but his friend.

"She ain't just no pig, Pa," he had said. "She en Oscar are my best friends. They's my family, just like you en Momma."

C.J. looked at his teenaged son, who still had the mindset of a young child, and realized that if he ever did any harm to the animal, the boy would not forgive him.

"No changin' what you can't change," he placated himself. Then he chalked up Minnie's expenses as just a part of life you had to accept. Minnie not only remained with them, but she was no longer bred.

Presently twenty-two, Tubby, had only gotten out of high school two years before in 1974. Although he had started school with the rest of the kids his age, because it hadn't been discovered that he was developmentally delayed, he had been held back in first and second grade. By third grade, his situation was identified and he was put into special classes.

When Tubby was in grade school, it was hard on him socially. First he was a large boy and, being held back, made his size even more obvious. It was also difficult for him to make any friends, because the other students would move on and he wouldn't.

But even in the best of circumstances, it wasn't as if there was a line of kids waiting to befriend him. Quite the contrary. Most made fun of him by teasing him about his big, burly, and burr-cut head. They also teased him about his baggy overalls, and the pig poop, crusted boots he liked to wear. Almost daily, they told him he stank which deeply hurt his feelings. He would go home in tears and cry to his momma.

"Tubby, everyone and everything in God's big world is different," she told him. "Nobody knows why we are like we are, but believe me, there's a reason for it. Ain't ours to question and one day those little children you go to school with, will figure that out. Just you wait and see," she patted his head. "You have your own unique purpose and it's something that no one else on earth can do but you. You be proud of that, ya understand?" She took his chin in her hand and lifted it, making Tubby look her in the eyes.

"I guess so," he acquiesced, but he wasn't sure.

However, time reveled that Myrtle had been right. When Tubby got a little older, the teasing mostly stopped because of a popular boy named Vincent.

Vincent, seeing Tubby alone at lunch one day, made a special effort to talk to him. He left his table of popular kids and went to sit with Tubby. The rest of the room turned to witness it, mouths gaping.

"Hey there," he said, taking a seat next to Tubby. "I'm Vincent. You're Tubby right?"

Tubby nodded yes.

"Mind if I sit here?"

Tubby shook his head no.

"So you got some meatloaf huh?" Vincent asked, pointing to the red and brown glob on Tubby's plate.

Tubby spoke. "Yeah, I likes it. It ain't as good as Momma's, but I still thinks it's good."

Vincent laughed. "Yeah, it's not half bad. Not real fond of the peas though." He made a face.

Tubby took a big fork of them and shoved them in his mouth. "I like em," he said, revealing the half eaten vegetable.

"Well they say they're good for you, so good for you!"

Tubby laughed. "That was funny – they're good for ya so good for ya!" he snorted.

Vincent stayed at Tubby's table and made small talk. He asked Tubby about himself, including where he lived, what he liked to do, and if he had any brothers or sisters.

Tubby got a forlorn look in his eye when Vincent mentioned his family.

"I had a sister once," Tubby acknowledged, "but she died the day she was borned. My momma cried a lot," Tubby bowed his head, remembering.

"I'm sorry," Vincent sighed. "That happened to my mom too," he revealed. "It happened before I was born though."

"Not me," Tubby answered. "I was 'bout five. Momma showed me where my sister was livin' in her stomach. She'd let me talk to her and tell her stories. But she didn't breathe when she came out. Momma said God decided he needed her ta live with Him instead a us. I wondered if it was because I wasn't going ta be a good brother, but Momma said that wudn't it. I'm not sure though," Tubby bit his lower lip.

"Naw, Tubby," Vincent reassured him, "that wasn't it. You would have been a great big brother. I'm sure of it."

Tubby smiled and nodded his head. "Yeah," he said proudly, "I wudda been a great big brother."

Once Vincent had given him the okay, the other kids in school instantly joined suit, and when Tubby saw them at lunch, they all would turn and greet him.

"Hey Tubby, how's it going?" one would smile. Tubby waved and smiled back.

"Having a good day?" another would ask, and Tubby would nod his head. Tubby kept a grin the size of Dallas on his face most of the lunch hour because of the attention he would receive and, when he was with his classmates from the Special Education class, Tubby would introduce them to the other students. This made Tubby somewhat of a hero to the kids in his class.

Tubby liked to eat lunch with his classmates, but at least once a week, Vincent convinced him to stray from his group and join him. The invitation was always the same.

"Hey Tubby," Vincent would wave to the burr-headed boy, as soon as he had gotten his tray. "We gonna eat lunch together today?" Then he would slap the seat next to him, motioning for Tubby to sit.

"Sure Buddy," Tubby grinned as he walked to the table.

During the lunches, Tubby told Vincent tales about Minnie, Oscar, and the other animals on the farm. He relayed how it was his job to take care of the pigs, and get the eggs from the chickens.

"They squawk at me like they's mad," Tubby revealed, "but the very next day, they's got more eggs just waiting for me, so I don't think they really care."

Vincent would listen with great interest, then nod and laugh when Tubby told some of his stories. He actually snorted milk through his nose the day Tubby told a story of finding a chicken snake in the hen house.

"It scared me so bad I wet my overhauls! Momma said it wudn't a hurt me, but I don't believe her," Tubby squinted his eyes together, searching Vincent's face to see what he had to say about the subject.

"She's right Tubby, Chicken Snakes don't bite. They just eat eggs."

Vincent's assurance seemed to greatly relieve the boy.

"Man, that's good ta know. It was big enough ta eat me whole!"

Vincent laughed. "Yep they can get pretty big all right. I'm glad you were okay though, Tubby."

Tubby grinned like the Cheshire Cat, revealing the spaghetti he was eating.

"I like eatin' with ya Vincent. Ya makes lunch purty fun."

Vincent smiled back at the boy, who sometimes smelled more like pig dung, than he did boy.

"I like it too Tubby. You make me laugh and that's a special thing. Let's make a pact that we'll do this until we get out of school okay?"

"Issadeal," Tubby nodded his agreement through a huge piece of bread he had stuffed into his mouth.

It was obvious to anyone who cared to pay attention to the boys' relationship, that although they were both so different, they had something very profound in common. Both had hearts that were made to love others. In fact, it was Vincent who made Tubby realize, that what his momma told him when he was younger, was true.

"Momma," Tubby said to her one day after having had lunch with his friend, "yous was right about everybody having their own purpose en it bein' something that no un else on earth cud do but them."

Myrtle stopped crocheting the potholder she was working on and put it in her lap. "That right?"

"Yep," Tubby said, as he sat down beside her. "And I know why Vincent is here. He's here ta be my friend, en there's nobody that kin do it as good as him," Tubby smiled.

"I'm glad that you see that, Tubby," His mother returned the smile. "Vincent *is* a good friend. You make sure and tell him okay?"

"I will Momma, but he knows it 'cause I already told him so."

It was true. There hadn't been a lunch since the very first one, when Tubby failed to tell Vincent what a good friend he was. Vincent would slap Tubby on the back and return the compliment.

"So are you buddy, so are you."

Chapter Four

Tubby's real name was Martin, but from a baby he had been roly-poly, so his mother nicked named him Tubby. It was really all he ever remembered being called.

From the time Tubby was very small, it was clear he had a way with animals. His father marveled at the way his son seemed to communicate with them. It made no sense to him how the small boy could tell him – a man who'd been around a farm and its animals all his life – that a horse's hoof was cracked.

Tubby was only about five when he had followed his father into the barn and tugged on the man's pant leg.

"Daddy, JoJo's foot hurts 'em."

C.J. ignored the boy, thinking he was playing make believe. The following day when Tubby had again come to him, tugging on his overalls and repeating the warning, C.J. asked him why he thought it was so.

"He told me," Tubby replied, as if he was confused that his father hadn't been told too.

C.J. looked long and hard at the boy, but something in his eyes revealed that Tubby wasn't playing make-believe. With Tubby tagging along behind, C.J. headed toward the small corral. He climbed the pipe fence and walked over to the gray colored horse. He took the horse's face in his hands and looked him in the eye.

"You got a gimp foot JoJo?" he asked the gray gelding.

JoJo stared back, not answering. C.J. took JoJo's nose and pulled it to the left, trying to get the horse to walk. JoJo followed him but winced with the second step.

C.J. looked over at his boy.

"It's his back un Pa," Tubby said, pointing to the animal's left hind leg.

C.J. looked at the boy again, wondering how he could possibly know that, but he chalked it up to Tubby just paying more attention to the old horse than he had.

C.J. patted JoJo, reassuring him that he had no reason to fear him or possibly kick him before he walked to the horse's flank and bent down to examine the leg. It looked fine. Then he looked at the hoof. There was a crack at the front toe. C.J. sighed.

"Oh boy, just what I need, a lame horse." He stood up and looked over at his boy.

"Let's get em in the barn and out of this wet mud," he told the youngster. It's too damp for him ta stay here and we don't want this ta get any worse than it is."

Tubby ran to barn and retrieved JoJo's bridal and bit. He brought it back to his father who slipped the bridal over the horse's head and the bit into his mouth. Tubby looked up at his beloved friend.

"Don't ya worry, JoJo, Pa's going to fix you right up. Aren't you Pa?" He turned to look up at this father.

"Gonna do the best we can," C.J. tried to reassure them both.

JoJo snorted and nuzzled Tubby, before the father and son led him into the barn, and into his stall.

"We gonna have ta keep him here awhile until I get him fixed up. Think I can fix this with some clamps or sutures. I'll ask Doc Downing his opinion first," C.J. scratched his head. "In the meantime, JoJo," he looked at the horse, "I guess you are on vacation."

Tubby was petting his friend, barely able to reach his neck.

"Hear that JoJo? Ya don't have ta work none!"

The horse again snorted at the boy.

"He says that makes em happy," Tubby reported to C.J. "And he said ta tell ya thanks!"

C.J. shook his head. His boy had some imagination on him.

"Come on, let's ride inta town en talk to Doc Downing; see what he suggests," he motioned for Tubby to follow him.

Tubby obliged, but not before standing on his tip toes and giving JoJo a kiss on the storm cloud colored hair of the animal's nose.

"We'll be back real soon to fix you up, JoJo."

JoJo nodded and snorted again.

Throughout his life, Tubby had thought that everyone could talk to animals like he could. It wasn't until he and his father had a showdown, when he was not yet ten, that he learned his abilities were actually a gift.

Tubby had come in from fetching eggs that morning, and told C.J. that a chicken hawk had been snatching some of the baby chicks.

C.J. questioned him.

"Tubby, how did you know that it was a chicken hawk that was getting' the chicks?"

"'Cause Reddy told me Pa," he answered, as if the family's rooster relaying such a message, made all the sense in the world.

What do you mean Reddy told ya?" C.J. cocked his head with a quizzical look.

"I mean when I was gettin' the eggs, Reddy come up ta me en said a chicken hawk had got three a the chicks en I needed ta keep them inside the wired pen til they gots bigger."

C.J. shook his head, trying to find the words to explain to his son, that his make believe stories needed to stop. But before he scolded Tubby by telling him he was too old to be pretending anymore, a thought occurred to him.

How had Tubby known there were three chicks missing? He hadn't been home two days before when C.J. noticed that two of the babies were gone. Tubby had left before sunup to go on a school field trip to the Oklahoma City Zoo and he hadn't returned until around eight that evening. That was long after his father had already locked the birds up for the night. But, just the previous afternoon, again while Tubby was away at school, C.J. had actually witnessed the hawk making circles around the free range area where the chickens tended to scratch and wander. He had watched helplessly as the bird swooped in and grabbed a third chick.

As C.J. sat with the boy and with Myrtle at their breakfast table, he couldn't come up with an explanation as to the real way Tubby had known about the hawk. He was sure though, that it wasn't because Tubby could communicate with animals.

"Tubby, I'm not sure how ya knew there was a hawk, considering that ya were gone all of the other day, but I don't think Reddy told ya about it. At any rate, you're a big boy now and it's time ta stop all the foolishness 'bout talkin' ta the animals. Tell me how ya really knew, because people can't talk ta animals, Son. It's impossible."

Tubby cocked his head to one side and furrowed his brow.

"No it ain't, Pa," he shook his head. "How kin it be impossible when I does it all the time? Surely ya kin talk to 'em too?" He looked questioningly at his father. "Ya talks ta Oscar. Ya ask him how he's doin' en he tells ya he's good."

Tubby turned to his mother. "Momma, ya tells Yeller Cat ta get off the sofa, en she tells ya she don't want ta, en ya tells her again, en she will," he reasoned.

Myrtle looked at C.J. who returned the stare.

"Son, I don't hear her tell me she don't want to. I just tell her to get off again because she hasn't done it the first time."

"Ya don't hear her when she answers ya?" Tubby's eyes grew wide.

Myrtle shook her head.

"Pa, ya don't hear Oscar tell ya he's doin' good?"

"No Son, I don't, and you don't either. It's just make-believe," C.J. reasserted.

Tubby jumped up and put his hands on his hips. His face got bright red in anger.

"That ain't true. I do hear 'em'" he stomped his feet. "I hear Oscar, en Yeller Cat, en Reddy, en Minnie, en JoJo, en all the chickens, en…" Tubby began to cry. "It ain't make believe Pa!" he wiped his nose with the back of his sleeve. "I'll prove it ta ya right now. Come with me ta the barn." Tubby headed toward the door.

C.J. tried to protest but Tubby was already outside and down the steps. He strode to the barn with a purpose like no other C.J. had witnessed before. C.J. looked at Myrtle.

"Come on Momma; this ought ta be good," he exhaled, and helped his wife to her feet. They followed their son across the yard to the old barn and entered.

"I wasn't gonna tell ya 'cause Pearl told me she wanted it ta be a surprise," Tubby addressed them, while pointing to a scruffy goat that was housed next to Minnie. "She's gonna have some babies."

C.J. laughed. Even if he had, for a split second, actually entertained the idea that his son might be able to talk to animals; he now had the proof that it was indeed just the boy's imagination.

"Tubby, there ain't no way this goat is gonna have babies. We don't even have a billy goat right now, for her ta mate with," he waved his arms through the air, motioning to the empty stall next to the nannie goat.

"She ain't having babies with no billy here," Tubby pointed his finger past his father. "She's having babies with Mr. Fife's goat Bud." Tubby put his hands on his hips. "She told me so this morning," he turned to the nannie goat. "Didn't you Pearl?"

"Baaaaaagh," Pearl said, and she looked to the ground, sorry she had been found out.

"I don't understand what you're trying ta say, Son. Pearl can't be havin' babies with Bud because Mr. Fife and I ain't got 'em together. I know she was in heat a couple a days ago, but I don't want no more mouths ta feed right now and I didn't make any arrangements ta mate her," C.J. put his own hands on his hips, as if he had finally proven his point.

Tubby started to counter, when the group heard a truck coming up the driveway. They left the barn and saw Mr. Fife's old sky blue ford pickup sputtering up the half dirt, half gravel road. C.J. turned to look at Tubby, then he looked at Myrtle. His eyes grew wide.

Bernard Fife stopped the truck and killed the engine. He swung open the door, which creaked like it needed a pint of oil, before slamming it shut again and extending his hand to C.J.

"Hey C.J, how ya been?" he tipped his old ball cap to Myrtle and nodded at Tubby. "Don't mean to intrude on ya, but figured I better get on down here and tell you what happened yesterday," he took the cap from his head and wiped his brow as if trying to buy himself some time.

"Late yesterday afternoon, I saw that Bud wasn't nowhere to be found and I started lookin' for 'em," he chewed on his lip for a moment before continuing. "Couldn't find him round the house so I started checkin' the pastures. Finally saw him coming back through yer fence there," he pointed to the east fence of C.J.'s property.

C.J. followed his neighbor's finger. He saw that the bottom two rows of barbed wire had slid to the ground, creating a large section where almost any animal – much less a small goat – could enter and leave as they pleased.

C.J. looked back at Bernard. Mr. Fife continued his confession.

"Think my Bud got together with your nannie," he sighed. "He was sure a happy feller when he got back. Just thought I should let ya know so you could get your fence fixed and so you wouldn't be surprised a few months from now."

C.J. looked at Myrtle then at Tubby before finding a voice to answer.

"Well thanks for comin' down here and lettin' me know, Bernard," he extended his hand again. "If she has a litter, you want some of 'em?"

"I wouldn't mind taken a few off yer hands," he nodded. "They keep the back pastures mowed down pretty well. Keeps the field mice at bay."

The two men continued the conversation for a moment longer as Tubby headed back to the barn. He went straight to Pearl's pen.

"See, it's okay Pearl, Pa's not mad. Some of the youngins are gonna get ta stay with Bud en some with yous. That'll be good won't it?"

Pearl bleated again.

Tubby heard his father and mother enter the barn. C.J. cleared his throat. He didn't have the words he needed to address what had just occurred, because again, Tubby had been at school all day and there was no way he could have known about Bud and Pearl's rendezvous. He stood looking at his son for a moment. Tubby returned the gaze, as if to say *"I told you so."*

"Tubby, um," C.J. struggled with his words. "Tubby, how long did ya say you've been able ta communicate with these animals?"

Tubby stood a little taller, realizing that his father no longer thought he was making it all up.

"As long as I kin remember Pa. I thought yous en Momma cud too." He kicked the dirt.

"No Son, we can't," C.J. looked at Myrtle, who was shaking her head no. "I don't know of anyone who can, do you Momma?"

Myrtle shrugged. "No."

"As long as I've lived, I've never heard of anyone who can talk ta animals Tubby and I don't want ya ta think..." C.J. struggled with his words again. "I don't want ya to think we think it's bad or anything, but ya can't tell anyone else that ya can do this. They won't believe ya."

Tubby looked into his father's eyes, not understanding why people wouldn't believe him.

"Pa," he protested, "why wudn't they believe me? I don'ts lie. I knows some people think I'm different, but theys don't think Ima liar do they?"

"No Tubby, they don't think you're a liar," Myrtle stepped forward. "Everybody knows you're a good boy. It's just that people don't believe what they can't understand. Like your daddy told ya, we've never heard of anybody – in all our lives – who can do what you can do. People fear things they can't explain. Fear has a funny way of making people do some terrible things, honey."

Myrtle walked to the boy, took him by his shoulders, and looked him square in the eye.

"Fear is a demon that can change a weak and timid soul into a heartless and unrecognizable monster. You must never tell a soul, or you could be hurt. Do you understand me Tubby?"

Myrtle held Tubby back and looked at him long and hard. "Do you understand that you are never, ever to tell anyone what you can do?"

Tubby half opened his mouth, but nothing came out.

Myrtle began to shake her son's shoulders and Tubby's knees began to shake with them.

"Tubby?" she got closer to his face. "Tell me you understand me."

Tubby finally nodded his head. "I understand Momma. I won't tell anyone."

It had more than a dozen years since C.J. had learned of Tubby's abilities but, he had never gotten comfortable with it. It still took him by surprise when Tubby would come to him and disclose that one of the animals had a problem or a request. In fact, it was still his first inclination, to dismiss it. However, when he did, Tubby was adamant and would pester his father until he was able to convince him to attend to the matter at hand.

That's exactly how it had been when Tubby first told C.J. to stop breeding Minnie.

C.J. wasn't going to give the request a second thought until Tubby cornered him one night at the dinner table.

"Pa, I told ya that I don't want ya ta breed Minnie anymore en I want ya ta promise me ya won't," he eyed his father seriously.

That's when C.J. told him that having more piglets was Minnie's job and she had to earn her keep. Tubby's reply was almost more than C.J., and Myrtle, who had been listening keenly, could handle.

"Pa, ya remember when Momma had my sister livin' in 'er stomach en yous, en Momma, en me was excited 'cause she was going live with us en be my sister?" he asked the already weary man.

C.J. cleared his throat. Just the mention of the subject sent a pain through his heart like he had not experienced since the day their daughter was stillborn. He sat another moment before regaining his composure enough to reply.

"Yeah Tubby, I 'member it."

"Well I knows Minnie's piglets are breathing when they is born, en I knows she gets ta stay with 'em for a while, but as soon as you take 'em away, her heart feels like it will explode. She says she would rather die than lose 'em again. She can't bear it Pa," he leaned into his father and looked him in the eye. "If ya gonna breed 'er, ya gotta let her keep her babies," he declared.

C.J. sat in silence for a moment. Myrtle, with a small tear forming in her eye, dabbed at it while using her other hand to pat C.J.'s knee under the table. C.J.'s silence led Tubby to believe that his father was not going to abide by his wishes so he reemphasized the situation.

"Just like when God took our baby from us ta live with Him, en we got sad en Momma cudn't stop cryin', that's what Minnie does. Please Pa," Tubby was now pleading more than demanding, "don't make her suffer like Momma did, okay?"

C.J. took a deep breath, exhaling it slowly. "I understand," he solemnly nodded. "Minnie won't be bred again, Son."

C.J. then got up from the table and went into the trailer's small bathroom. Tubby heard the man blow his nose and he looked at his mother.

"If I cudda told God not ta take your baby, I wudda Momma." Tubby bowed his head and sighed. "He might a listened ta me, en yous en daddy wudn't a been so sad."

"It's okay sweet boy," Myrtle looked at her son. "I don't think it works that way with God. He has His reasons and He knows best. I know I'll learn those reasons someday and it'll all make sense then." She stroked Tubby's chubby face.

"I'm gonna go tell Minnie the good news," Tubby, now excited, arose from the table. "Is that okay Momma?"

Myrtle nodded her head and rose too. She headed toward the bathroom to check on her husband and offer whatever little comfort she could.

Chapter Five

Tubby loved summer time. He often rode JoJo through the pastures to the South Canadian River and then back again to his farm. He and JoJo would stand on the bank's edge and look down across the wide river, which was dry sand most of the time.

C.J. had warned his son long ago that he was never to get off the horse and climb down the steep banks to play there.

"There are pockets of quicksand all over that river son, and they will catch ya like the fly paper catches all those flies; and it won't let go of ya," his father explained. "I would never find ya and that would break mine and your momma's hearts. Ya understand?"

Tubby agreed to follow his father's orders; still he wondered what it would be like to explore the dry bottom, especially on days when he had seen others do it, like the group of teenagers he witnessed playing chase underneath the big bridge that led to Maiden. Even though he wanted to obey, his curiosity could get the best of him. He was sure there would be treasures to find amongst the fallen tree trunks and debris. Sometimes he tried to convince JoJo that it would be okay to go explore – for only a moment, but JoJo never allowed it.

Tubby also liked to go look at the river after a hard rain – a toad strangler his father called it. The water would rush by in torrents, carrying more broken tree limbs and other vegetation. He often saw it carry large fish by too. It amazed Tubby how different the exact same scene looked when water was added to it.

On those days, JoJo would make sure to stay further back from the bank in case it decided to give way from all the rain. His protectiveness made Tubby feel loved, and for his whole life, he had trusted JoJo completely.

Tubby had never known a time without JoJo by his side, as he was at least five years older than Tubby. Tubby respected JoJo's wisdom and his unique perspective about life on the little farm and, he had been seeking his counsel since he was old enough to toddle.

For instance, when Tubby was about nine, he got very upset when his father took several of their cows to market to be sold. He went to JoJo, tears streaming down his face.

JoJo took the opportunity to explain to Tubby that everyone and everything had a purpose and that purpose must be served.

"See Tubby," JoJo looked at his red faced and sniffling young friend, *"we are all the same on the inside. We are all just souls with different coverings."* He watched Tubby to see if he understood. Tubby blankly blinked so JoJo continued to explain.

"We all have souls and before we come to live here on Earth, we pick our coverings. It's like when you change clothes," he nuzzled Tubby's overalls.

"I likes my overhalls the best," Tubby told JoJo, who laughed.

"I know you do. I like them for you too. But what I'm trying to say is, although you wear your overalls, you are not the overalls right?"

"I guess so," Tubby tried to follow JoJo's logic.

"No, you are Tubby inside of overalls."

"Oh yeah," Tubby smiled and nodded.

"See, I'm not just a horse. I'm a soul that chose a horse covering. Oscar is a soul that chose a dog covering. Minnie is a soul and she chose a pig covering. And you and your mom and your dad are souls that chose human coverings. Does that make sense?"

Tubby smiled widely, "Yeah, I get it!"

"Well at the same time that we choose our coverings, we choose our purpose. We each choose to take on a mission that will help others. It's why we are all here." JoJo paused to make sure Tubby was understanding. When he saw Tubby was still attentive, he continued.

"A lot of the animals decided to come here to be of service to humans. Take me for instance. You won't remember it probably, but before your dad got that tractor, I helped him plow the fields. After he got the tractor, I helped with other things like carrying things that were too heavy for him."

Tubby sighed and kicked the dirt.

"Why's Oscar here?" he asked.

"He's here to be your best friend. He's here to show you how wonderful you are."

Tubby smiled and bent down. "Awww," he said to Oscar, who had been sitting beside the boy and was also listening to JoJo.

"What about Minnie?" Tubby asked, tilting his head toward the pig sty where Minnie was laying in the mud.

"Minnie offered herself to serve in whatever way she was most needed. She didn't really know exactly how she would be used, but she was willing to come anyway. She is very special because she was totally selfless," JoJo explained.

"What does selfness mean?" Tubby asked his equine teacher.

"It's selfless," JoJo corrected, *"and it means that someone is willing to completely forget about their own wants and needs in order to provide for another. It's how we should all strive to be."*

"I don't like it when 'er babies have ta leave," Tubby pouted. "She doesn't either."

"I know. It has been hard on both of you. But Minnie does it to help others. She is selfless and it's her way of showing perfect and unconditional love. That is what we are to strive to do."

"But it makes 'er so sad," Tubby reminded JoJo.

"It's okay to be sad. It means that we loved. And Minnie may not always remember this, but deep inside her soul, she knows she didn't really lose her babies. They may have sacrificed their lives to be food for humans, but it is what they

chose. Even though their bodies died, their souls didn't, because souls last forever, and Minnie will be with them again at some point."

"I wudn't wanna be food," Tubby kicked the ground again.

"I understand," JoJo affirmed. *"but the animals understand the bigger picture. It is only when humans disregard an animal's sacrifice, take it for granted, or treat them badly, that there is wrong doing."*

Tubby furrowed his brow, showing JoJo he didn't comprehend.

"Many years ago," JoJo continued to explain, *"the natives of this land needed to hunt bison, and deer, and other animals, in order to survive. Although they would take the life of an animal for food, clothing, and other things they needed for their lives to be easier, they understood that everything has a soul – even the rocks – and they respected the Earth and all she provided for them. If they killed an animal, the first thing they did was thank it for its sacrifice, and they honored it, and sent its soul away with love and respect."*

Tubby scratched his head and chewed on his lower lip.

"They did?"

"Yes, Tubby they did."

JoJo looked at the animals around the farm and Tubby followed his gaze.

"Somehow though, people have forgotten that an animal's sacrifice is to be honored. They have forgotten they should be grateful. Instead, people began treating animals as if they had no value other than the meat they could provide. They lost sight of the soul inside."

"I don't thank the animals I's eats. I guess I's been takin' 'em for granted too." Tubby hung his head remorsefully.

"Like I said, most have forgotten," JoJo replied. *"But, they should be reminded. They need to understand that it is a great act of love to die for the sake of another. It is the most holy and pure thing a soul can do, and it should be recognized as such."*

"I will make sure en do it from now on. I will make sure that Momma en Pa do's it too. I promise," Tubby pledged.

"That's good Tubby. I'm glad you are willing to acknowledge the gifts you have been given."

"What about the animals we don't eat?" Tubby perked up, eager to learn from the wise animal.

"Well, if souls elect to come here as another animal, it is usually so that they can experience what it is like to be that animal. After they themselves observe the hardships or

difficulties it takes to exist as that animal, they can have more compassion and, they can better appreciate that animal during later lifetimes. If everyone could learn to see life through the perspective of others, we would literally have Heaven on Earth."

JoJo could see that Tubby was struggling with what he was imparting.

"Think about before you met Vincent. What did you think about him?"

Tubby shrugged. He had seen Vincent ever since he was in first grade when he and Tubby were in the same class. Vincent had lots of friends on the playground and little girls would pass him notes. They would giggle and huddle as he walked by.

"Did you like Vincent?" JoJo broke into Tubby's thoughts.

"I don't think so," Tubby scratched his head. "He had a lot of friends en I didn't, en I wanted friends too. I wanted ta be like em," Tubby twisted his mouth and grimaced before he settled on his answer. "No, I didn't like em," he confessed. "He had what I's wanted en it made me mad."

"What changed that?" JoJo questioned.

Tubby looked at the dirt in thought. "When he came over en talked ta me. He told me he had a sister that died too. He told me that my sister didn't die because I wudn't a been a good brother. He said I wudda been a great brother." Tubby shook his head up and down in agreement with the thought.

"See, it was only after getting to really know who Vincent was that you could let your anger go. You saw that he wasn't anything like what you thought. Isn't that right?"

"Um hmm," Tubby nodded. "I really liked 'em. He was a good person. I felt sorry that I thought bad 'bout 'em."

"See Tubby," JoJo nodded himself, *"in almost every case when someone doesn't like another, it is because of who they believe that person is, and not because of who that person really is. Commonality is the first seed of love."*

Tubby looked at JoJo, bewildered.

"Commonality means that we recognize something we have inside ourselves, in somebody else. It shows us that we aren't really different after all. It doesn't matter if you are an animal, a human, a rock, or a plant; we all have something in common if we will just take the time to look for it," JoJo smiled. *"When we recognize ourselves in others, we can begin to love them."*

JoJo took his nose and brushed Tubby's arm. *"Like you and me Tubby; we both like to go to the river and we like carrots and apples!"*

Tubby laughed. "Yeah! En Oscar likes ta snuggle, en he loves beef jerky, just like me!" Tubby grinned. "En Minnie likes ta hum, en she will eat anything, like me!" Tubby jumped a little with excitement, but then he stood perfectly still, engrossed in his next thought.

"I don't know 'bout a rock though," he eyed JoJo, challenging him to answer.

"Well, that's a little more difficult, but what if I told you that everything that you see, including yourself, is really just a bunch of the tiny things that make up both of you?" JoJo said motioning to everything around them. *"And what if I told you that we are all made up of the same exact tiny little things?"*

Tubby shook his head no. "That don't make no sense JoJo," he scoffed.

"Okay, think about this. You know how you and your momma like to do puzzles?"

Tubby nodded.

"Well if you just have one piece of the puzzle, you don't know what the picture is do you?"

Tubby shook his head.

"But what about when you put the whole puzzle together?"

"I kin see what the picture is!" Tubby exclaimed.

"That's right. And believe it or not, you are like that puzzle. You are really a bunch of itty bitty tiny little particles put together to make the whole picture of you."

Again, Tubby shook his head no.

"Yes Tubby it's true. Right Oscar?"

Oscar smiled his agreement.

Tubby looked at Oscar like he had been betrayed. "No Oscar," he said.

"It is that way Tubby. It is!" Oscar wagged his tail.

"How? I'm all in one piece. I ain't got no puzzle pieces." Tubby twirled around and showed himself off to his two pals.

"Tubby do you remember when you told me that you got to use a microscope at school?" JoJo asked.

"Uh huh," Tubby answered.

"Remember how you said that you looked at part of a leaf and you said that when you looked at it without the microscope that it looked like a leaf, but when you looked at it under the microscope, it turned into those little round things with dots in the middle?

"Yeah."

"That's what I'm talking about," JoJo said. *"Those were cells you saw, and there are millions and millions of them that made up that one leaf. Inside those cells are even smaller parts called atoms and even though cells are not in everything, atoms are. Everything in the entire world is made up of atoms, even the rocks!"*

"Wow," Tubby let his mouth hang open. "Yous has Adams? I has Adams? Oscar has Adams en rocks have Adams?" Tubby marveled.

JoJo laughed, *"Yes except they are called A Tom's not A Dams."*

"Oh," Tubby sheepishly grinned.

"And it's more than we need to discuss today, but all our atoms vibrate with energy and even they have parts that are smaller. But the bottom line is everything you see is made up of the same thing; it just takes a different form depending upon how fast or slow it vibrates. You don't need to worry about any of that though."

Tubby nodded his head.

"Some other day, I'll tell you how we are all connected too, but for now...," JoJo tilted his head and looked hard into Tubby's face, *"just remember we are all the same. And to finally answer your question about what you have in common*

59

with a rock – you know how sometimes you just want to go off on your own and sit quietly so you can think about things?"

Tubby again nodded.

"That's what it's like to be a rock."

JoJo saw the understanding arise in Tubby's eyes. "I'm gonna do that now JoJo," Tubby sighed. "I'm gonna go be a rock so's that I can think 'bout all this. Come on Oscar, yous be a rock with me."

Tubby and Oscar headed to the small pond over the ridge and there Tubby sat, Oscar by his side, until the sun went down.

Chapter Six

Before Tubby found his self-worth from Vincent, he had found it in Oscar. After a long and extended rain, several of the back roads had washed out leaving school buses unable to pass. Tubby had to walk about a half a mile from his house to the main paved road in order to catch the bus.

One drizzly afternoon, after the bus had dropped him off at the gravel road that led to his house, Tubby began walking home. He had only gone a short way when he heard a whimper in the tall brush beside the road. Tubby cautiously approached the area, but heard nothing more. He stood there for another moment, wondering if his ears were playing tricks on him. Suddenly, he saw the brush move slightly. He backed away for a moment, afraid that the movement may have been one of the many things he was afraid of, like skunks, opossums, armadillos, or snakes.

Tubby heard the whimper again, but this time, it didn't cease. He knew instantly that whatever the animal was, it was hurt and that gave him the courage he needed to investigate.

Tubby took two steps to the edge of the road and parted the shoulder high weeds. There below him lay the black dog, who was clearly still a pup.

"Oh no," Tubby bent down to look at the wet and shivering animal. "What's wrong? What's wrong with ya doggie?"

Tubby stuck his hand into the brush so that the dog could smell him. The dog looked up at him with the saddest eyes he had ever seen. Before Tubby even realized what he was doing, he set his satchel down and scooped the dog into his arms. Although the animal was small, Tubby at only six-years-old, wasn't much larger.

The dog bore his shivering body into Tubby's chest and sighed. Tubby wrapped himself around the animal, picked up the satchel, and struggled with his load as he walked home. Along the way, he softly soothed the frozen puppy.

"As soon as we git home, I'll gets ya a warm bath. Ma'll get ya some warm milk too," he told his new friend. "I'll take the best care of ya that ya's ever seen. You kin sleep with me too."

The dog no longer whimpered, but instead, looked up into his new boy's eyes, in unadulterated adulation. It was only moments before he yawned sleepily, and closed his dark eyes. Tubby smiled to himself when the dog began to lightly snore.

When Tubby made it home with his new best friend, he opened the door to the little white farm house and dropped his satchel inside the door. Then he went around to the back of the house and quietly snuck up the stairs of the back porch. He opened the door and looked around. Tubby sighed in relief that his mother was nowhere to be seen. He crept through the kitchen and into the bathroom. He closed the door and sat the dog on the floor. Then, he began a thorough investigation of the animal's body.

Everything looked fine until he got to the dog's underbelly. A small, thin, but bloody slit, shown on his chest. Tubby gasped. He looked under the sink and found an old washcloth. He wet it and then sat down beside the dog and gently lifted him onto his lap. The puppy opened his sleepy eyes.

"What happened Doggie?" Tubby whispered. "How'd ya get this here cut?"

The dog licked Tubby's hand. "Awww, I likes ya too," Tubby told the furry creature.

"Ya don't say?" Tubby listened as the young hound relayed how he had been thrown out on the side of the road by the people who owned the place where he'd been born. He told Tubby that a large and jagged piece of gravel had cut him when he landed on the road.

Tubby gasped. "Was yous the only one?"

The dog said that his brothers and sisters were also dumped, but each in a different area.

"I was the last one they put out," he sniffed. *"They said they didn't want us. They said my mom shouldn't have gotten herself mated. I don't know what that means. I miss my mom."* The animal lowered his head and whimpered.

"Don't you worry," Tubby assured him. "You's gonna live with me en Momma en Pa. We has lots a other animals too. Is that okay with ya?"

The dog licked Tubby's hand again.

"Let's git ya cleaned up."

Tubby began gently cleaning the wound and found that it had long stopped bleeding but the rain and wetness had made it look fresh.

"How long was ya out there?" Tubby crinkled his brow in worry.

"Since last night," the pup answered.

Tubby took the mutt's head in his hands. "I'm so sorry." A tear slid down Tubby's cheek and his lip began to quiver. "I'm so sorry that ya was treated that way. It don't make no sense that someone'd do that to yous, en yous brothers, en yous sisters."

The dog nuzzled into Tubby and laid his head across his lap. In his mind he showed Tubby a picture of his mother. *"Don't let me forget what she looks like,"* he said.

"I won't," Tubby kissed his head.

The next thing Tubby knew his mom was shaking him.

"Tubby, why are you asleep on the bathroom floor?" she asked her boy. She lifted his head and saw the black mass beneath it.

"What in the world?" Myrtle bent down to get a closer look. "Oh no you don't Tubby Anderson. We are not keeping that dog. Where in the world did you find him?"

"Momma, we have ta keep em," Tubby bellowed. "He don't have no place ta go. Some bad people threw em out down the road. They threw his brothers en sisters out on other roads. Look Momma, they hurt him!" Tubby picked up the pup to show his mother the dog's belly.

"You can't just throw em out again. He's not trash," Tubby implored. "He's alive like yous en me. He wants ta stay with me. He wants ta live with us. I already told em he cud!" Tubby frantically tried to make his case. "He's still a baby Momma. He can't take care a 'emself."

Tubby began to cry as snot ran down his nose. He took the washcloth and raked it across his face before pleading some more.

"Momma, we can't let em think everyone's as mean as those bad people. He'll make us a good pet. He'll be my friend. He loves me already, don't you…?" Tubby stopped his tirade, realizing he didn't know the dog's name.

"What's your name?" he asked the dog who was panting from all the excitement.

"Oscar," he answered.

"Momma, Oscar loves me en I love him. He has ta stay with me. I can't live without em."

Oscar got up off Tubby's lap and went to Myrtle. He stood up on his hind legs, coaxing her to pick him up. She looked down at him, his red tongue hanging out, and tail wagging. Then he licked her shin.

Myrtle stepped back, trying not to succumb to the magic spell being placed upon her. She looked at the door, almost willing C.J. to find them and put his foot down. In fact, she knew that if he didn't come through the door in the next couple of moments, they were about to own a dog.

"See Momma!" Tubby got to his feet. "Oscar loves ya too!"

Myrtle looked to the ceiling. "Oh my Lord, I do not want to keep this dog," she sighed.

"Please Momma, please!" Tubby begged.

Oscar now sat his rump on the floor and smiled at her.

Myrtle looked to the ceiling again, trying to summon every ounce of energy she had to say no. She looked back at the dog, ready to pronounce him banned, but what came out of her mouth was nothing near that.

"You have to take care of him," she told Tubby.

Myrtle could not believe what she had just heard herself say. She tried to take it back, knowing full well that she was going to have to deal with C.J., and realizing that it would be next to impossible to justify what she had done. But Tubby was already jumping up and down. He had picked up Oscar and was hugging and kissing him.

"I will Momma. Thank yous, thank yous, thank yous!" Oscar plied Tubby with kisses and Myrtle shook her head.

"God what have I done?" she asked, backing out of the bathroom. "And Lord, what am I going to tell C.J?"

Myrtle turned around and closed her eyes. She took a deep breath and shook her head in disbelief. *"How will I ever tell C.J.?"* she asked again, before leaving the new friends to bond even more.

From that moment on, both boy and dog were inseparable. Tubby relied on Oscar as much as Oscar relied on him. And unlike most children, who pledge to care for a pet before immediately abandoning their promise, Tubby was true to his word. He made sure each and every day that Oscar had plenty of food and fresh water. He also let him out, took him for walks and cared for him if he was sick.

When Tubby was at school, he would count the hours until he was reunited with his perfect pal, and in turn, Oscar would be waiting at the end of the driveway for Tubby to exit the school bus. As soon as Tubby unloaded his satchel, the two would begin their adventures of trekking through the woods and playing their favorite game of treasure hunting.

Since the day he had found an arrowhead and some shards of pottery in the far edge of the property near the river, Tubby was convinced there was treasure on the property.

Especially during the summer, Tubby liked to take his mom's hand shovel, a paper sack of snacks and his beloved dog, and set out to explore any place he hadn't already been.

"We's gonna find lots a good stuff," he would tell Oscar, who agreed whole-heartedly.

The boys would be gone from the moment Tubby finished chores, to long after their tummies had told them that they missed lunch. Sometimes, they would indeed, find good stuff.

One of Tubby's most memorable finds was a mouse skeleton which had been buried under thick wet, leaves at the base of a giant cedar. Oscar had been the one to alert him to it, while nosing through the fallen leaves that had settled under the evergreen.

"Look Tubby," he got his friend's attention. *"I haven't ever seen anything like it."* Oscar pointed out what was left of the small creature.

"Whoa," Tubby's eyes got huge. "That there's a skeleton. There's one in Mr. Thorn's class. I sees it when I go by for lunch. It scares me," Tubby backed a step away.

"Yeah, but this one can't hurt you," Oscar wagged his tail. *"It's too little."*

Tubby stood a moment thinking about what Oscar said. "Yeah, you's right," he agreed, stepping up beside his friend. Tubby pushed the dark green-blue foliage aside and got down on one knee to examine the bones more closely.

"Wadda ya think it was?" he asked Oscar.

"Don't know," the dog answered, *"but it can't be a dog like me. It's too little. Can't be a cat either."*

"Or a pig, or a horse, or a chicken, or a duck, or a cow, or a..." Tubby looked up at the sky, trying to think of other animals he knew.

"Nope, none of them," Oscar agreed.

"Let's take it to Pa. He'll know. Pa knows everything about everything." Tubby nodded his head.

"Yeah..." Oscar agreed with the same admiration Tubby had for his father, *"he knows everything."*

Tubby scooped up the small creature and the two ran as fast as they could back to the barn.

"Look Pa," Tubby yelled before even seeing the man. "Look whats we got!" He ran inside the barn and found his father shoeing JoJo.

Tubby held out his hand and showed his father their find.

"Got yerself a mouse skeleton do ya?" C.J. said, while examining Tubby's hand.

"Ohhhh," Tubby looked at Oscar, who was panting heavily, his tongue was hanging out of his mouth. Oscar wagged his tail.

"That's what this here is – a mouse?"

"Yep, that's what it is," C.J. had turned back to his work.

Tubby looked at Oscar again who woofed. *"That's neat,"* he smiled at his friend.

"Pa ya think there's other skeletons on this here land?" Tubby's eyes grew wide. "Like people ones?

"I seriously doubt it, Son," C.J. answered, without looking back.

"Ya sure?" Tubby sounded worried.

"Well, not exactly." His father stood up from his stooped position and looked at his boy. "You know there have been people on this land for lots of years before we got here. Back in the day, people were buried where they died and the Indians lived all around here. I doubt they's any burial sites around here though 'cause we wudda seen signs of it. They took good care of their people when they passed." He paused for a moment in thought. "But like the bible says Tubby, 'Ashes to ashes, dust to dust.'"

"Huh?" Tubby tilted his head, bewildered.

"'In the sweat of thy face shalt thou eat bread, till thou return unto the ground; for out of it wast thou taken: for dust thou art, and unto dust shalt thou return,'" C.J. quoted.

Tubby stared blankly at his father.

"Even the dirt you're standing on used to be a part of somebody."

Tubby looked to the ground, and when he realized what his father said, he started trying to get off the dirt. He finally found a hay bale nearby and jumped up on it.

C.J. laughed. "Tubby, ain't no escaping it. We are all going back to the earth when we die. No one gets outta here alive."

Tubby didn't like it when there was talk about dying. It gave him a weird feeling in his stomach and it made his heart beat fast. Sometimes, he would even feel like he was going to throw up.

C.J. saw the angst on his son's face, walked over to him and sat down beside him on the bale of hay.

"Dying ain't something you gotta worry about for a long, long time," he patted Tubby's leg. "But at some point, we all gotta do it. Dying is just another step in living – just like eatin', sleepin', and breathin'. 'Cept we only have to die once," he chuckled.

"I don't wanna die. I don't want yous ta die, I don't want Momma ta die," Tubby started to tear up.

"I know you don't, but that's being selfish. This here life is sometimes hard, Son. People wear themselves out trying to tame things they ain't ever gonna tame. Why we do it, Heaven only knows, but for some reason there's a callin' in us that makes us labor and toil. But Tubby, there comes a day when we can't do it anymore; we gotta rest. That's when we get ta go home and be with everyone we love that's already gone on," he shrugged. "So when the time comes for me and your momma to go, you gotta be happy for us. You gotta understand that we are bein' rewarded for all our hard work and sacrifice. God's gonna tell us 'well done' and let us back in the fold."

Tubby looked up at his pa, a big and sorrowful frown adorning his face.

"Tubby, I'm not saying that you can't be sad. Of course you will be. You are gonna miss me and you are gonna miss Momma, but you are just gonna have to remind yourself that it won't be forever. You will be with us again someday and until that day, we'll be looking out for you just like we do now,"

C.J. bent his head over to look into Tubby's eyes. Then he smiled.

"Good news is it ain't gonna be for a long, long time. So no worries okay?"

Tubby nodded his head, but he didn't really feel better. He got up and motioned for Oscar. The two went inside and pulled out Tubby's secret box from under his bed. It was where he stored his most prized possessions.

Somehow, the excitement of finding the skeleton had lost its luster and the boys curled up on the rug beside the bed. Tubby thought about his father's words.

"I want it ta be forever 'for Pa and Momma leave me Oscar."

"Me too," Oscar answered.

The two laid silently looking at the ceiling until they both drifted off, the soft snoring of Tubby, replacing his worry.

Chapter Seven

The fear of death was a reoccurring theme in Tubby's life, most likely because he had been confronted with such a permanent loss at a young age.

After his sister was buried, Tubby often dreamed of the little casket being lowered into the ground. He remembered seeing the tiny, lifeless child at the funeral home. He had actually touched her, his hand recoiling at the coldness of what should have felt like skin, but instead felt like rubber. He wondered where she had gone.

Although his parents had tried to explain the concept of Heaven, God, angels and such, any true understanding had eluded him.

He often talked to his animal friends to try and better understand it all. In fact, he and Oscar had spoken about it at length throughout Oscar's time with him.

"Whyda ya think my sister didn't breathe?" he asked one evening as the two had settled in for bed, Oscar curled next to him.

"It isn't for us to know Tubby," Oscar told him. *"And you shouldn't be spending your time wondering about it because you are missing out on what's really important."*

Tubby cocked his head to one side. "Wadda ya mean?

"People have a bad, habit of living in the past and it's the greatest waste of time and energy there is."

"Wadda ya mean?" Tubby asked again.

"Tubby it's been a long time since your sister died hasn't it?"

"Yeah."

"But you've spent a lot of time thinking about it, haven't you?"

"I guess so," Tubby shrugged.

"Did any of that time you spent thinking about it change it? Did your sister come back to life? Did it change your momma's sadness or yours?"

"I don't think so," Tubby cocked his head to the other side.

"Now think about that time. Is it ever coming back to you? Can you grab it and stuff it in your pocket and use it later?"

Tubby didn't reply, thinking about the idea.

"You can't Tubby, it's never coming back and therefore it is time that you wasted. Think of all the great fun we have every single day. If you knew that I would be gone in a short time, what would you give to still have more time with me?"

"Anything!" Tubby sat upright and grabbed Oscar's head in his hands. "I would give up everything I gots, includin' our secret box. I'd give up everything in it." He looked Oscar in the eye.

"Now what if you could look back at our time together, or your time with your ma, your pa, JoJo, Minnie, or any of us, and you could see how much time you spent worrying about things in the past that you could never change. What if that time added up to years? How would you feel knowing that you let years get by you that you didn't get to appreciate what you had right in front of you?"

Tubby lowered his head and crinkled up his face. He wanted to cry.

"See Tubby, most people actually spend years thinking about the past. They spend years of their limited time worrying about tomorrow. Unfortunately, very few ever really live in the here and now. They miss the best part of life, which is right in front of them. It's not just the big things either."

Oscar looked up at the boy he loved more than anything in the world. Then he laid his head across Tubby's lap.

"You remember when we got to see that butterfly come out of its cocoon?" he asked.

"Um hmm," Tubby nodded.

"You remember how neat it was? You said it was one of the neatest things you had ever seen."

Tubby nodded again.

"It's those kinds of things people miss each day. They may go for a walk, but they are so consumed with thinking or worrying, they completely miss it. People miss the vast majority of their own lives because they don't know how to live in the present moment. And you know what?"

"No," Tubby answered.

"The saddest part of life isn't when someone dies. It's when they never lived."

Tubby took a deep breath and then sighed.

"I had just been here worryin' 'bout my sister, en before that I was wondering who I was gonna' play with, en I missed bein' here with yous," Tubby started to sniffle.

"Don't cry Tubby," Oscar licked Tubby's hand. *"Just promise that from now on, you're going to let the past stay where it is, and let the future take care of itself."* Oscar smiled at his boy. *"It can, you know. It's been doing it for billions of years, and no amount of worrying about it is going to change how it will unfold."*

Tubby nodded and wiped his nose on his sleeve.

"I loves ya Oscar."

Oscar smiled and stuck out his tongue.

"Enough to give me some beef jerky?" He raised his eyebrows.

Tubby laughed. "Yeah, I'll get ya some beef jerky."

"Oh and Tubby?"

"Yeah?"

"I love you too."

"Enough to share?" Tubby laughed, and Oscar laughed too.

"Always."

Tubby tried to train himself not to think about the past but it wasn't easy. Once he realized he was doing it, he would remind himself about the conversation with Oscar.

He also tried to not worry about the future, although that seemed even harder than forgetting the past.

One night when Tubby had already been tucked in and his wise dog lay beside him, he asked Oscar what he could do to stop worrying.

"It's pretty simple really," Oscar looked at him. *"Once you realize that the only reason you try to know the future in advance, is because you are afraid of it, then you can begin to control it."*

"I don't understand," Tubby said with a shake of his head.

"People only worry because they are afraid," Oscar reiterated. *"Here's the really sad part of it Tubby – they make themselves afraid over something that isn't real. No matter what scenario they come up with in their mind, it won't be what really happens – ever."*

"I don't thinks that's right Oscar," Tubby disagreed.

"Why do you say that?" Oscar got up and put his head on Tubby's stomach.

"'Cause one time I was worried that I was gonna get a spanking 'cause I took Pa's screwdriver after he told me not ta mess with his tools. I lost it. I knew the next time Pa needed it, en it wasn't there, I was gonna git in trouble. I knew he'd spank me – 'cause he told me he would, when I lost a tool before. He did spank me Oscar!" Tubby sat up in the bed.

"Okay," Oscar acquiesced, *"But do you remember when you worried about it?"*

"Yeah," Tubby replied.

"Tell me what, in your own mind, you thought was going to happen."

"Well I thought that Pa was gonna fly off the handle en be so mad that he would strap me good."

"How long did you worry about it?" Oscar asked.

"It was a couple a weeks 'cause he didn't need the screwdriver til then."

"What happened when he found out you lost it?"

"I was talking ta JoJo in the corral en Pa hollered at me ta come ta the barn. He asked me where his screwdriver was. I was so scared I cudn't answer him," Tubby remembered.

"Then what?" Oscar coaxed.

"He asked me if I had taken his screwdriver en lost it. I told him I did, en he told me ta go git a switch off the tree. I started crying en told him I was real sorry, but he told me I still had ta go git it, so's I did," Tubby looked at Oscar, forlorn.

"And?"

"And he give me three switches," Tubby frowned.

"Okay, now think about this Tubby, was the spanking as bad as what you thought it would be?"

Tubby sat in silence for a moment remembering the event.

"Nah," he swung his legs over the bed, then petted Oscar. "I thought it was gonna be a lot worse."

"And how did you feel when it was finally over?" Oscar asked.

"I was glad. It was like I wasn't so heavy anymore," Tubby tried to explain.

"So you spent two weeks not being able to enjoy your life because you were worried about something that wasn't real," Oscar nosed Tubby's hand, trying to get him to pet him.

"I did!" Tubby was stunned at the realization. "I spent all that time bein' worried. I didn't even want ta eat so's you know I was feelin' bad."

Tubby looked down at Oscar and sighed. "Even though I gots a spankin' it wasn't bad at all," he confessed.

Tubby laid back on his bed, mulling over all he had just discovered. Oscar broke into his thoughts.

"Tubby, fear isn't real," he reiterated. *"It's a sad thing because people give it all their power. They let it make all their decisions for them. The worst part of it is that if they didn't allow fear to be a part of their decision making, they would make totally different decisions than what they make. That means, they can't live the life they want because they are afraid."*

Tubby sat up again and looked at his advisor.

"See Tubby, people know in their hearts why they come here to Earth. They feel it – they have a passion for it. But most ignore it because they or someone they love, convinces them that they can't make a living at it, or that they won't be good at it, or that it's silly. So instead of doing what they really want to do, they find something else that fits the idea of what they think is secure." Oscar looked at Tubby to see if he was following. Tubby seemed to be deep in thought.

"I loves animals," Tubby mused. "I guess ya cud say I's got a passion for 'em," Tubby smiled at Oscar.

"Just like your momma says, 'Passion is God's whisper you are doing what you came here to do.'"

"I spend almost all my time with yous guys," Tubby acknowledged. "Does that mean I'm doing what I'm 'posed ta do?"

"There is no doubt about that. When you are with us, you are doing exactly what you came here to do," Oscar licked his friend's hand.

"I'm glad," Tubby replied, rubbing his eyes and yawning. "'Cause I loves you guys." Tubby petted Oscar's head before lying back on the bed.

"You guys are my best friends," he sleepily proclaimed. "I'm glad you's the reason I'm here," he yawned again.

"Me too Tubby," Oscar lay down beside the boy. *"Me too."*

Chapter Eight

Tubby heard his mother calling from the back stoop of the trailer. He turned back to Minnie.

"I gots ta go see what Momma wants. Ya gonna be okay?" he asked the listless creature.

Minnie nodded and Tubby left her to check in with Myrtle.

"I need you to go into town and get a few things," she told her son.

"Momma, ya knows Minnie's real sick. I can't leave her," he protested.

"I'll watch over her and it won't take long. I just need you to go to Ralph's Grocery and get some bread, then to Stephen's Drugstore and get you some Odor Eaters. I cannot stand the smell of your feet one day longer," she frowned.

"Momma," Tubby whined, "I don'ts wanna leave Minnie."

"You do what you're told Son," Myrtle took a stern stance with her firstborn.

Tubby kicked the dirt and mumbled something about it not being fair. "Let me go en tell Minnie that I'll be gone for a bit," he reluctantly agreed.

"Minnie, Ma is making me go inta town en git some stuff. I won't be gone long. Is it okay?" he asked the ailing sow.

Minnie grunted her agreement.

"I'll be back as soon as I kin," he petted her head before turning to leave.

When he got to the door, he turned back to her. "I loves ya Minnie," he half-heartedly smiled. "You's the bestest pig in the world."

Minnie raised her head and smiled at him. *"You're the bestest boy in the world,"* she sighed, and that made Tubby smile.

Tubby went back to the trailer to get the keys to the pickup truck. His mother handed him two dollars which he stuffed into one of his overall pockets.

When he got to town, he parked between the drugstore and Ralph's Grocery. *"I'll get the bread real fast,"* he surmised *"that way I kin get to see that purty girl at the drugstore longer."*

Tubby had developed a crush on the girl the very first time he had seen her. She worked behind the soda fountain and he thought she was the prettiest girl he had ever seen. He ran into Ralph's, grabbed the bread and paid for it as quickly as he could. Then he threw it into the cab of the pickup and bounded down the street to the drugstore.

He spotted the cute blond as soon as he entered the store. He stopped at the soda fountain and addressed her.

"You're purty," he smiled.

The girl looked him over and backed away before thanking him.

Tubby took her thanks as a good sign.

"We should go onna date."

The girl shook her head a little before replying.

"I have a boyfriend," she whined as if annoyed.

Tubby wasn't about to let another boy stand in the way of his happiness.

"I kin beat him up. Who is he?" Tubby smiled again so she would see how much he liked her.

"In the first place," the girl backed away a little more, "I don't want you to beat him up, and in the second place, it's none of your business who he is." The girl scowled but Tubby didn't take notice.

"You're purty," he repeated, trying his best to impress her.

"Thank you," the girl groaned while rolling her eyes.

Tubby remained oblivious to the fact that the girl was not interested in him in the least. Instead, he formed his perfect plan.

"We cud go ta the movie," he suggested, remembering that Vincent had once told him that the movie was where all the kids went on their dates.

"In the first place," the girl shook her head, "I already told you I have a boyfriend. And in the second place, I have already seen the movie."

Tubby was sure that if the girl just got to know him, she wouldn't like her boyfriend anymore. However, to be sure, he tried again to convince her he was a much better choice.

"I kin beat him up," he repeated, while showing her his muscle.

The girl huffed in dismay. "I'm pretty sure we already covered that," she rolled her eyes again. "I am not going out with you Tubby, and I have work to do, so you need to tell me what you came in here for," she demanded.

Tubby became very excited. He hadn't known that the pretty girl knew his name. That had to mean that she liked him because he didn't even know her name!

He grinned.

"My ma says I need Odor Eaters 'cause my feet stink. Want ta smell?" He tried to balance on one foot and pull his boot off the other.

"No," she answered, backing away even more. "I'm sure your mom knows what she's talking about. Do you want me to get them or do you want to get them yourself?"

Tubby told her he would go so that he could see all the colors of the medicine bottles which lined the walls. He told her his favorite was Listerine.

"You use Listerine?" the girl asked, as he walked to the adjacent aisle.

"Nope," Tubby informed. "I just like the color. It looks like pee!" Tubby was sure the girl would find him extremely humorous.

Tubby looked at the bottles as he passed. He saw the pee colored Listerine and a dark blue bottle with Phillips on the label. He also saw a pink one that he recognized as Pepto-

Bismol, which his mother would give him when he had a stomach ache.

As he eyed the pink concoction, he accidently farted and it wasn't inconspicuous. In fact it sounded like an oversized, tailpipe on a Harley Davidson motorcycle. It was one of the better farts Tubby had let in his time and he was proud of it. In fact, he hoped to himself that the blond girl heard it, because he knew she would be impressed. Just in case she hadn't, Tubby alerted her.

"I farted!" he yelled to her over the aisle.

"Yeah Tubby, I kind of figured," came her reply.

Tubby was even more proud when he found out that it was so loud the girl heard it.

"Whew," he bragged, "that was a good un! I mean bad un!" he countered when he got a whiff of the stench surrounding him.

"Tubby," he heard her say, "I don't need a play by play!"

Tubby got more excited when she again called him by name.

I kin tell she likes me," he told himself. *"I can't wait ta tell Minnie!"*

The girl interrupted his thoughts. "You need to get your Odor Eaters and go," she ordered him.

Tubby was unsure as to why she sounded mad at him but, he looked around, finally spotting the Odor Eater rack. He looked them over, seeing both blue and black ones, but having no idea which ones to get.

"Have you found them yet?" the girl yelled across the store.

"Yep," Tubby answered. "But I don't knows if I should get these here blue uns or these here black uns."

At first, his love didn't answer, but after a moment she yelled back to him.

"Get the black ones. They're for men. The blue are for women."

"Well that makes sense," Tubby thought to himself. *"Blue should be for women 'cause it's purty."*

Tubby took the Odor Eaters to the cash register at the soda fountain. He looked at the girl again, thinking she was truly the most beautiful thing he had ever seen. He handed her the item and grinned – extra wide, so she would see how much he liked her. She ignored him, and asked him for two dollars and fifty-two cents. Tubby handed her his money.

"Tubby, I need a dollar and forty-nine cents more." Tubby noticed she had turned her face away from him. Tubby was sure that she didn't want him to see how much she liked him too. Vincent had told him that girls liked to act like they didn't like a boy when they really did. "Hard to get," he had called it. Tubby sheepishly grinned again, although she couldn't see it.

"I ain't got it," Tubby held out his hand to show her he had nothing more. "That there is all Ma give me," he nodded to the money and gave her his famous puppy dog look that made his momma give him anything he wanted.

The girl starred at him for a long moment before she threw up her hands. "Take them and go," she waved him off and then grabbed her nose.

Tubby wondered if it itched, but not before realizing that his charms had worked. After all, she didn't make him pay for the balance of the foot pads.

Tubby knew, like the girl had said, that he needed to go so he could get back to Minnie. However, before he left, he figured he better inform her of his future whereabouts so she could find him. He knew she would be breaking up with her boyfriend since she had discovered his interest.

"If ya want ta go out with me, I'll be back here next Saturday," Tubby alerted her.

"Tubby, just take your Odor Eaters and go! How many times do I have to tell you I have a boyfriend?"

Tubby was momentarily confused. Surely she was breaking up with the other fellow. Just in case, he felt he should remind her of his attributes.

"I kin…"

"I know, I know…" she interrupted, before grabbing a can of Lysol and aiming it at him, "you can beat him up. NOW GET!" she yelled, pointing him toward the door.

If there was ever a doubt that this girl loved him as much as he loved her, it was demolished with that act.

"She wants to make everything smell good for me," he whimsically told himself before exiting the store and skipping to the truck.

Chapter Nine

Tubby went back home and straight to the barn to check on Miss Minnie. She was asleep so he bent over and kissed her on the snout. The he sat down on a small wooden stool that he and his Pa used to milk their cows. It was mid-morning and the sun was already announcing that the day would be unseasonably hot. Myrtle and C.J. called the hot fall days, "Indian Summers." Tubby didn't know why.

Minnie had been feeling poorly for a few days and Tubby couldn't figure out why. The day he first noticed it, he wasn't overly concerned. Considering it had been hot so far in the fall, Tubby assumed that the heat may have been getting to her. Heat was hard on older pigs. But, when the following day she didn't eat but a bite or two of the scraps he had thrown her, he knew she was sick. He stayed with her most the rest of the day.

The following morning, when he finished his chores, he headed back to the barn to stay with Minnie. He had given her little drinks of water, but she no longer would eat. Tubby feared the worst.

Tubby watched his companion of several years, as her belly heaved and recessed with each breath. He loved her with all his might. He hated this part of caretaking. He had already had to say goodbye too many times in his young life.

One day, as he sat beside his beloved dog at their favorite summer spot on the bank of the pond, he asked Oscar why animals did not get to live as long as humans. When Oscar explained it, Tubby knew he was right.

"It's harder to be an animal than it is to be a human," Oscar had said. *"Humans have a lot of things that make life easier on them. They have houses, and cars and machines that do their work. Plus they can take care of themselves most of the time."*

Tubby listened intently before commenting.

"Yeah but wild animals can take care of themselves," he countered.

"Yes they can, but they still have a very difficult life," Oscar looked up at Tubby. *"If they want to eat, they must hunt. But worse, if others want to eat, they are hunted."*

Tubby frowned.

"Their homes are not like yours, where you have heating in winter and cooling in summer. God designs their bodies to adapt to temperatures, but still, most of their time here, they are uncomfortable."

Tubby lay back on the grass, contemplating what he was hearing.

"Also," Oscar educated his young companion, *"animals always live in the moment. They never live in the past or the present, so it is as if they really live longer than humans."*

Tubby raised back up and looked at his dog. "I don't understand," he crinkled his face.

"Remember when I explained how much time humans waste by living in the past or worrying about the future?" Oscar reminded Tubby.

"Yeah," Tubby answered.

"Well, because animals never waste time and live in the exact moment they are in, they really live every second of their lives. Humans only live a fraction of their time here. So in real

present time," Oscar tilted his head, *"animals live as long or longer."*

"Ohhhh," Tubby displayed his understanding.

"If humans lived in the moment like animals," Oscar continued, *"their lives would seem like they lasted hundreds of years."*

A squirrel, descending a nearby oak tree, caught Oscar's attention and he bounded from the boy's side. He made a beeline for the tree, while at the same time barking frantically. The squirrel ran back up the tree and immediately began chastising the dog. Oscar laughed before returning to Tubby and laying his head on the boy's lap.

"Anyway," he continued, *"because it is harder and because we live more fully, animals get to return sooner,"* he yawned.

Tubby stroked his head and fondled his floppy black ears.

"Are all animals the same?" Tubby questioned.

"No, not really," Oscar answered, *"but most are more aware than humans."*

"Wadda ya mean?"

"Well most humans – not all – don't come here knowing their purpose. Animals do. Souls choose to incarnate as animals when they are at a level of awareness that makes them

want to develop their compassion. They come here so that they can feel what it is like to be an animal, and thereby be more loving and helpful the next time around."

Tubby scratched his head. "I still don't get it," he sighed.

"Every soul's ultimate purpose is to learn to love unconditionally. Do you know what that means?" Oscar asked his friend.

Tubby shook his head no.

"Well, if you love someone unconditionally, it means that no matter who they are, what they do, what color of skin they have, how much money they have, or even if they have been mean to you, you will still love them with no strings attached. Part of loving others unconditionally is being of service to them too." the black dog rolled over so he could look at Tubby and have his belly scratched at the same time.

"It also means that you will treat everything in the world – no matter what it is – with love, dignity and respect. It means you can recognize the spirit within all things. It means you understand that everything is connected and all part of the One."

"One what?" Tubby frowned.

"One Divine Maker," Oscar smiled. *"Every single person and every single thing, is just one small part of the Creator."*

"I'm not followin' ya," Tubby flatly starred.

"Okay, you know how this pond is made up of water?" he asked the hefty child.

"Uh huh."

"Well, what if I got just one drop of water from this pond. Is it still water?" Oscar asked.

"Yeah," Tubby answered.

"Is it still a part of the pond?"

"Yeah."

"That's right," Oscar wagged his tail. *"See, God is the pond, and we are all just single drops of water from that pond. We may be separate sometimes, but we are still a part of the pond, we are still a part of Him."*

"Oh I get it now!" Tubby grinned.

"Pretty neat huh?" Oscar asked, and Tubby agreed. *"So back to the animals. When a soul comes here as an animal, they come with the knowledge that they are not separate and they come here without egos."*

"What's an ego?"

"That means that, unlike humans, animals already know they are perfect and they don't need to rely on anyone else to give them value. Does that make sense?"

Tubby bit his lip in thought. "I'm not sure."

"Well, you remember when you thought you needed the other students at school to like you before you thought you were likable?"

"Yeah."

"Animals don't need that. We know we are perfect. See, in that sense it is harder to be a human than an animal, because humans don't remember they are perfect and so, they sometimes spend their entire lives trying to become something they already are. It's like when I chase my own tail," Oscar laughed. *"I never catch it! I just go around in circles and I don't get anywhere. It's still fun though,"* he chuckled.

Oscar then became more serious.

"I don't think it's fun if you're a human though. I think it's sad. I see you are perfect. I see that everyone I meet is perfect, but they can't see it. It's one of the reasons souls come here as humans, so they can remember it and learn to rely on God for their value instead of others. Others really have no idea who they are," Oscar sighed. *"I don't know why humans allow people, who don't even have the faintest idea who they really are, to determine their worth. It just doesn't make sense."*

Tubby rolled over to face his companion. "You's right Oscar," he told the dog. "Those kids at school didn't know me at all. The only people who really knows me is Momma, en you guys." Tubby motioned to the animals scattered around the small farm. "En yous guys are the ones that loves me most. So's I don't know why I wanted people that didn't knows me ta decide 'bout me. It *don't* make sense!" he slapped his leg.

Oscar jumped to his feet and licked Tubby's face. *"I do love you!"* he slobbered.

Tubby laughed. "I'll try'n remember that I'm perfect," he wiped away the slobber and grinned.

"If you don't, I'll remind you." Oscar licked his boy from chin to forehead again.

"Okays Oscar. Thata be good."

Chapter Ten

From the stool where he sat, Tubby continued to watch Minnie's slow and shallow breathing. For as much as he knew, Minnie had lived a wonderful life. She had a nice place to live, plenty of food, and more love than she could have ever wished for. Tubby also knew in his heart, that it was her time to leave it all behind, and return to her Maker. Still, it didn't make his sorrow any easier.

In a way, Tubby had felt as if Minnie had been his own child. From her birth, they had never spent a day apart, not to mention that he had actually carried her in his overalls until she was too big. He understood that a large part of his heart would be missing as soon as she left.

His mother called out to the barn at noon time. "Come on in Tubby. I got lunch ready for ya."

Tubby wasn't willing to leave Minnie's side, even for lunch.

"I gotta stay here Momma," he yelled back at her. "Minnie's still sick."

Myrtle brought him a sandwich and some milk. He half-heartedly picked at it, offering Minnie a bite every so often, which she refused.

Tubby remained inside the pen the rest of the afternoon, talking to Minnie when she was awake and even when she wasn't. As he watched her sleep, he remembered how difficult it was for her during the first few months of her life.

Tubby had done everything he could to reassure the piglet that she was wanted and loved. He had exceeded in that task beyond anything Minnie could have ever hoped for but, after she was grown, she had told him that because she was not able to suckle for being pushed away by her siblings, she had not developed the same bond with her mother that they had. She told him that it made her feel like an outsider. Tubby lowered his head in sorrow.

"I'm sorry Minnie."

"Oh Tubby. Don't be sorry. Because you are what made it all better. I never felt that way when I was with you. The best place I've ever been was inside your warm and cozy bib,"

she relayed. *"I could hear your heartbeat, just like I heard my mother's while I was still in the womb."*

Minnie said it was the sound of his heart that she missed the most when she got too big to be carried.

A tear slipped down Tubby's dirty cheek as he thought about the role he had played in her life. He felt as if he had indeed, done something special for her with the love he provided. It was the perfect complement to the love she still felt for her pig family.

Although Minnie hadn't been as close to her mother and siblings as they had been to each other, she was still heartbroken when her siblings had to leave the farm. She would cry and Tubby would comfort her.

She was also devastated when her mother eventually passed. On the day it happened, Tubby sat up with her all night after her mother left.

Minnie, had laid flat on the hay, her head pressed hard against the ground, as she stared into a place only she could see. Tubby stroked her and kissed her head, telling her it was going to be okay. About three in the morning, Tubby, who had fallen asleep beside his precious friend, was awakened by Minnie nuzzling his face. She had burrowed her snout under his chin, trying to arouse him.

"Tubby, wake up! Wake up!" she implored.

"What?" Tubby sleepily mumbled.

"Tubby, my mom was just here," Minnie excitedly relayed.

Tubby thought he had not heard the pig correctly or that instead, he may have been dreaming, so he started to roll over and continue his slumber.

"Tubby, wake up!" Minnie demanded.

Tubby reluctantly sat up and looked at the pink animal.

"My mom was just here. She was right there," Minnie gestured to a spot a few feet from Tubby's head. *"She said she came to let me know that she was fine and that she would see me again,"* Minnie smiled.

Tubby looked at Minnie, still somewhat confused by the sleep that demanded its' due.

"Did ya say your mom was here?" he shook the haze from his head.

"Yes!" Minnie danced a little. *"She's fine! Isn't it wonderful?"*

Tubby, finally realizing what had happened, smiled too. He had been told before, by the other animals who had lost someone, that they also had been visited by the departed. The message had always been the same – they were fine, they were happy, they were at peace and, they would be reunited someday. Tubby had found great comfort in the reports, and it helped him more easily accept the temporary loss that he had to endure each time one of the animals left, or left someone behind.

Because he had heard it so much over the years, he found it very hard to doubt. So much so, that he often told his bereaved animal friends that they could look forward to it. He wasn't even surprised when those same friends came to tell him that a visitation had happened. Tubby delighted in the fact that each and every time, the visit had erased their sorrow, just as it had done that night for Minnie.

Tubby remembered how Minnie had continued the little dance that she had been doing, while speedily relaying to him the conversation she had with her mother.

"She said that some of my brothers and sisters were there too and that it was beautiful beyond my wildest dreams," she squealed. *"Oh and she was so beautiful Tubby! She was the most beautiful I have ever seen her,"* Minnie gushed before stopping her dance and looking into Tubby's eyes.

"She told me she loved me more than I could know and she would watch out for me," Minnie looked down at the ground reflecting upon her mother's words. *"She said she will*

always be with me – closer than she could have ever been in life." Minnie sighed before lying down beside her keeper and settling into him.

"That there's wonderful Minnie," Tubby smiled and scratched her ears. "I'm so glad ya got ta see her again."

Minnie rolled a little so that Tubby could rub her belly. *"Will you still stay with me?"*

"Yep," Tubby had replied as he situated himself beside her.

It was only moments before Minnie's warmth and contentment lulled him into a deep sleep, and only a moment more before the snoring of both boy and pig echoed throughout the otherwise silent barn.

Tubby knew that because Minnie was able to see her mother, it was making her own transition easier for her. She hadn't acted as if she had been scared of what she was going through at all. Tubby hoped that it would be that way for him too when his time came.

Although he had gotten much better at accepting the departures, he still struggled a little with the fear of it all. When he was younger, he feared death almost to the point of hysteria – especially after the tornado. Any little ache or pain signaled to him that he was dying. In his mind, a scraped knee could mean gangrene and a certain agonizing and slow death. A sore muscle meant cancer. Tubby even questioned if he had cancer when his mother shaved his head and he was bald.

He relentlessly cried one afternoon after Myrtle got the electric razor and buzzed his square and pudgy head.

"Tubby, what in tarnation is the matter with you?" Myrtle questioned when Tubby ran off to his room howling.

"Did I cut you Son? Come here and let me look."

Instead, Tubby closed his bedroom door and threw himself on the bed. Myrtle lightly tapped before opening it. Tubby was sobbing hysterically.

"Tubby what's wrong? Why are you crying? Are you okay?" his then frantic mother questioned.

"Ima not ready ta die Momma," Tubby wailed.

Myrtle took a step backward, unsure of why Tubby thought he was going to die. She almost began to panic believing that he might know something she didn't, but then she calmed herself in order to get to the bottom of Tubby's hysterics.

"What do you mean Tubby? Why do you think you are going to die?" The plump woman sat on the bed next to her son and rubbed his back.

Tubby rolled over to look at her, his face swollen face, and his nose red.

"'Cause I lost my hair like that woman we saw at Ralph's Grocery. Ya told me the reason she didn't have no hair was 'cause she had the cancer. Nows I don't got no hair so's I must have the cancer too," he wailed, his puffy cheeks turning as red as his nose.

Myrtle shook her head and sighed. "No Tubby, cancer doesn't work that way. Just because I shaved your head doesn't mean you have cancer. People who have cancer have to take medicine that makes them lose their hair. I only shaved your head 'cause it's summer, it's hot and you like play in the pond with Oscar. No hair means we don't have to shampoo you every time ya go swimmin'."

Tubby stopped crying. "I ain't gots the cancer?"

"No honey. Ya just have a burr haircut; nothing more." His momma smiled sweetly.

Tubby let out a big sigh of relief. "Good. I didn't wanna leave yous en Daddy. I didn't wanna leave Oscar, en Minnie, en JoJo neither," he sniffed.

"Oh honey," Myrtle ran her hand over Tubby's bare head, "you aren't goin' anywhere for a long, long time."

When Tubby had finally reached the age where all the animals were in his care and he had to say goodbye to them one by one, his thoughts about dying began to change. Each departure brought with it the heartache and gut wrenching pain, but it also brought a gift of solace in the messages and assurance that were sure to follow.

As Tubby watched Minnie's restless sleep, he remembered back to the first time he had to face the loss of one of his companions and when he learned that just because a body was gone, it didn't mean the soul was.

Donald was a Pekin Duck that liked to follow Tubby around, snipping at his heels for attention. Tubby would run from Donald, who chased him unmercifully, until Tubby went in search of June bugs or other tasty treats for him.

Tubby awoke one morning to find Donald laying still near the cattail reeds at the south end of the pond. At first Tubby thought Donald was a hen balled up unto herself, escaping the gusting March winds. However, the closer he got, he could see the curled drake feather and knew it was Donald. He then realized Donald was dead.

Tubby ran to the duck's side and picked him up, his neck dangling limp like a long blade of Johnson grass. He began to cry, as he looked around to see if he could find a reason for his friend's demise. He saw nothing that would explain the duck's death.

A few of the duck hens ventured toward the drake and Tubby when they heard Tubby crying. Nettie, the oldest of them, waddled to Tubby's side.

"He ate a coin," she told the boy. Tubby sniffed before looking down at her.

"What?" he tried to understand.

"He found a coin in the mud here," she said nodding to the edge of the reeds. *"We told him not to eat it, but he said it looked good and he swallowed it whole,"* she honked.

Tubby sat down with the deceased bird on his lap and stroked his lifeless body.

"He was always eatin' stuff he wasn't 'posed ta," Tubby sniffed. "I wish he wouldn't have done it," he choked a little.

Nettie sat down beside Tubby.

"After he died, he came back," Nettie told the boy.

Tubby looked at Nettie like she was crazy.

"You mean he didn't die all the way en woke up?

"No," Nettie shook her head, *"His body was still laying here by the pond,"* Nettie stated, as a matter of fact. *"It wasn't his body that came back, it was his spirit,"* she honked. *"He*

came when we were all in the barn." She looked across the pond to the barn.

Tubby sat in silence awhile, trying to comprehend what Nettie was telling him.

"That can't happen Nettie," he finally stated, looking down at her.

"Oh yes it can," she replied, nodding her head, *"because it did."*

Tubby waited for her to continue to defend herself, but when she didn't, he sat Donald aside and turned to her.

"I don't understand. How cud ya see him in the barn iffin his body was here dead?"

"I don't know," Nettie answered, *"but I did and so did the rest of the ducks."* She pointed toward the feathered crowd that was gathered. They all honked their agreement.

"He just told us that he was okay and that he was happy," Nettie continued. *"He said it was really great where he was and he would see us again."*

The ducks again affirmed Nettie's words with a chorus of honking.

Tubby shook his head, still not believing what Nettie said could be true. He had heard of ghosts although he had never seen one. Maybe ghosts were real.

"He was a ghost?" the bewildered child asked the hen.

"I don't think he was so much a ghost," she paused, thinking through her answer. *"I just think it was his spirit that came to tell us that he was okay and we shouldn't worry. I don't think he's here anymore like a ghost would be."*

The rest of the ducks nodded.

Tubby arose and gently picked up Donald's remains. He wiped his nose on his sleeve and stifled back more tears. "I'll gets a shovel," he told Nettie and the other fowl. "Let's go over there ta the hill en put him ta rest."

The ducks waddled that way while Tubby retrieved the shovel and returned to dig a hole to bury his feathered friend.

"This here is Donald," Tubby spoke aloud after placing the last shovel of dirt over the bird. "He was a good duck en a friend ta us all. He loved June bugs, en swimming, en helping the girls keep the babies close by."

The ducks looked at their friend's grave as another tear slipped down Tubby's round cheek.

"Ya'll want ta say sumpin?" Tubby asked the flock.

"We'll miss you, Donald," Nettie said to the ground where her friend laid.

The ducks nodded their agreement. Tubby did also, before they all silently turned away and waddled back to the barn.

Although he still sometimes struggled with it, because that same scenario repeated itself over and again throughout the years, Tubby was finally able to think about death without the all-consuming panic that once ensued. As he sat with his beloved Minnie, he thought about the faith he had developed, in believing that what all the animals had witnessed was real.

Even though he had never seen it for himself, he had a feeling deep in his heart, that what they told him was the truth. With that feeling came the hope that Minnie too would come back, and that he would be the one to see her.

Chapter Eleven

As he lay beside Minnie, Tubby thought about the reason he was still on the farm. He went through the long laundry list of reasons – the joy the animals gave him being just one.

"I loves my animals Momma," he had told his mother one morning at breakfast. "There's no place else in the world I wanna be 'cept with 'em," Tubby took a mouthful of bacon and chewed before realizing that his statement wasn't quite true.

"'Cept with yous en Daddy," he corrected himself.

His mother smiled. "We feel the same way about you, Tubby. There's nowhere else we want to be except with you." She buttered a slice of toast before acknowledging the love he had for the critters on the farm.

"I'd say that the animals are your passion," she handed the toast to him, "and you know that passion is God's whisper that you are doing what you came here to do," she smiled again.

"I knows I'm doing what I'm 'posed ta do 'cause I kin talk to 'em when no one else kin," he mumbled through a mouthful of food.

"It is quite a thing," Myrtle shook her head, still not understanding the gift that had been bestowed upon her son, but revering it just the same.

"As soon as Ima done eatin'," he smiled at his mother, "me, Beans, en Charlie's en Roscoe's two youngins, are goin' out past the pond to find Sheep Showers!"

Sheep Showers were clover sized and shaped plants, also known as Wood Sorrel, that grew wild in the spring. They were sour but tasty, and Tubby loved to chew on them as much as the goats did. The old timers would make Sheep Shower wine out of them. Tubby's dad had done it many times, although Tubby had not been allowed to drink it.

"Don't eat too many," Myrtle cautioned her son. "You don't want to get a belly ache."

"I won't Momma," Tubby agreed as he arose from his chair and headed toward the door of the trailer.

"Save some for your dad too," she hollered behind him before she turned to look at the boy. "And Tubby, you keep a good eye on them goats," she warned. "Don't want them getting across the fence and playing on Mr. Fife's stacked hay again – or worse."

The goats often found just the right place where the barbed wire slipped down a fence pole, allowing them to escape to the neighboring farm and engage in a somewhat comical game with Mr. Fife's small heard of goats. The goats loved to jump and spring off objects scattered near the barn.

Tubby would never forget the first time he saw it. He was walking back from the barn and noticed a goat flying through the air near Mr. Fife's barn. He wrestled his way through the fence in order to get a better look. As he approached the barn, he saw several of the goats jumping from hay bales, and careening off the side of his barn in pure and abandoned joy. The sight was so comical, he doubled over in laughter.

Tubby stood and watched as the goats, loudly bleating to one another, careened through what appeared to be an obstacle course that Mr. Fife had created for them. Tubby looked on in amazement as the goats jumped onto the hay bales, then hopped from one to the next, before running toward the barn. The goats actually defied gravity by running up the wall, and then flipping back to the ground. Once the course had been completed, each goat would get back in line to start all over again.

"Watchin' the goats?"

Tubby's trance was broken by Mr. Fife who was coming down the steps of his back porch, holding a large mallet in his hand.

"What's they doin'?" Tubby asked his senior neighbor.

"Oh they're just playin'," Mr. Fife had answered, as if it was the most natural thing in the world.

"They likes to play?" Tubby questioned.

"Oh sure," Mr. Fife nodded. "These goats live to play. I had no idea until I had laid these bales out to dry and I saw 'em start to climb and run across 'em. That one there," he said, pointing to a black and white billy goat, "that's Sir William. He jumped off one and ran to the side of the barn and did that flip thing and the other's followed suit. So I left the bales here and added some more so they could play all they wanted. Seems to make 'em better grass eaters," he added, scratching his head. "Guess all the playin' makes 'em awfully hungry."

Tubby was astonished. He had never seen his own goats do anything like it. "Kin I bring my goats over en see if they wanna play?" he asked the older man.

"Fine by me," Mr. Fife shrugged, "as long as none of mine are in heat. I got a few too many of 'em already." He eyed the line of goats in front of him.

Tubby left, crossed back over the fence, and collected Beans and Charlie. Beans was Tubby's billy goat and was aptly named because he loved beans more than anything.

If Tubby brought scraps with beans out to Minnie or the other hogs, Beans could smell them from across the yard. He would charge Tubby, knocking him over so that the beans would spill onto the ground. Beans would scarf the treat and immediately begin chasing Tubby for more – all before Tubby even realized what had hit him.

Charlie got her name because of her bleat. Tubby remembered when C.J. had helped Pearl birth three goats, one of which was Charlie. The moment she came out, she bleated "Ch-ch-ch-ar-ly."

"Hey Tubby," C.J. had turned to the boy who had been watching the birth, "I think you may be rubbing off on me. I would have sworn this kid just said Charlie," he scratched his head, bewildered.

"Yep," Tubby agreed. "I'm pretty sure she did."

"Well then, I guess you won't be the one naming 'er 'cause she has named herself," he shrugged.

Charlie was one of the nannies that currently lived on the farm. She was inseparable from Beans. She worshiped him like a teenage girl from the 1960's worshiped The Beatles. She refused to let him out of her sight.

"Come on ya two," Tubby motioned for the goats to follow him. "Mr. Fife's gotta great obstacle course for ya to play on."

Beans and Charlie did as they were told and followed Tubby to the fence. He held up the middle wire and stepped on the lower one so they could get through. Tubby and the goats walked the short way through the pasture until they came upon the goat playground.

Beans stood for only a moment, watching the fun the goats were having, before he ran to get in line. Of course, Charlie, would not allow him out of her sight, so she followed behind him.

Tubby watched in amazement as his two goats jumped and shimmied across the hay bales. He almost hit his knees in laughter when he saw Beans flip off the side of the barn. He did hit them when Charlie did the same.

"I don't believes it!" he laughed to Mr. Fife. "My goats kin jump en flip! Did ya see that?"

"Sure did, but it don't surprise me a bit," he clicked his tongue. "These critters are acrobats I tell you. Would of never thought it, but they are."

Tubby watched as his goats took their turn repeatedly. When it was beginning to get dark, he told the two they had to go home. Beans bleated his displeasure but Tubby insisted.

"You mind if I lets 'em come back en play sometime?" Tubby asked Mr. Fife.

"Not at all." he answered, "Just as long as my nannies aren't in heat," he reminded the boy.

Once the other goats on Tubby's farm learned of the fun, they demanded Tubby take them to play too. Tubby was a little apprehensive of taking Roscoe, the other billy, but Roscoe assured Tubby he would behave. Although Tubby took them often, apparently it wasn't enough because the goats disappeared from time to time leaving Tubby, C.J. or Myrtle scouring the farm to find them.

Invariably, they would be discovered at Mr. Fife's, playing. It wasn't a big deal until one of Mr. Fife's nannies came up pregnant after he had separated his own billys from them. The look on Roscoe's face when Tubby confronted him, revealed that he hadn't kept his word.

C.J. promised his neighbor that he would take the kids when they came, so Mr. Fife wouldn't have to care for them. He wasn't happy about it because he was hoping the six he had were going to be the last. However, after Roscoe's shenanigans, he was left taking care of three more.

It was true, Tubby loved his animals. He couldn't imagine his life anywhere else but with them. His greatest joy came from being their friend. His greatest knowledge of the world came from them also.

As he was about to graduate from high school, when others asked him what he was going to do, Tubby didn't understand their question. Being with his animals was all he had ever known and all he cared to know. What it would mean to leave, hit home with him hard when Vincent told Tubby of his own plans to leave after graduation.

During the last week of school, Vincent and Tubby sat on one of the benches in front of the school as they waited for their bus. Vincent told Tubby that he was going into the military.

"Tubby when you were just a kid did you play army men?" he asked.

Tubby got excited, "I wish I still did that; it was fuuuun!"

"Well I'm going to get to do it in real life."

"Tubby was jealous for a moment, thinking that maybe he should go too.

"Do ya gets ta take yous dog with ya?" Tubby asked his friend.

"Naw, they don't let you take your pets," Vincent answered.

Tubby sat in silence awhile, contemplating the idea. He couldn't understand how Vincent would willingly leave his Alaskan Shepard, Mush. The more he thought about it, the worse he felt.

"Aren't ya going ta miss Mush? Won't Mush miss yous?" Then it occurred to him that no one would leave their best friend so, Vincent must have been teasing him.

"Aw, you's just jokin'. "Ya ain't leavin' Mush – no way!" Tubby laughed and slapped his knee. "That was a good one, Vincent," he snorted and lightly punched Vincent's arm.

Vincent bit his lip, seeing that Tubby didn't understand.

"No Tubby, I'm not joking. I am leaving. I have to. I don't want to, but the Army isn't going to let me bring Mush."

Tubby furrowed his brow and shook his head no.

"Uh uh," he responded. "Ya don't mean it. Ya can't leave Mush. What's he gonna do?"

Vincent swallowed hard, unsure of how to answer. Tubby seeing his discomfort tried to reason with his friend.

"It's gonna kill em if ya leaves him Vincent. Please don't leaves him."

Vincent dropped his head in shame. "I have to Tubby," he whispered. "I don't have a choice."

"Yes ya do!" Tubby stood, put his hands on his hips, and looked down at Vincent. "Ya has a choice. Yous don't go! Yous stay here for Mush!" he ordered.

"Tubby, I can't. I have to go. It's what I'm supposed to do in life. It's where I'm supposed to be," he tried explaining.

Tubby continued angrily staring at his friend. Vincent tried again to reassure him.

"My mom, dad, and my brothers and sisters will take good care of him. And I'll get to come back and see him whenever I'm on leave."

Tubby still could not understand, because there was no way he would willingly leave any of his animals. He knew that they sometimes had to leave him when they were ready to pass, but he would *never* up and leave them as Vincent was planning to do.

That night at supper, Tubby, was still visibly upset.

"What's wrong, Tubby?" his mother had asked.

"Vincent is leaving Mush. He's going ta go play army men," he set his face in disgust.

Myrtle looked at C.J., an unspoken conversation playing between the two, and nodded for C.J. to take over.

"Tubby," C.J. began, "Vincent is doing a noble thing joinin' the army. Only the bravest of the brave are willin' ta do that."

"But he's leaving Mush!" Tubby didn't understand why his father didn't comprehend the severity of it.

"I know he is," he nodded his head, "but he has to. See Tubby, not everyone is 'posed to care for the animals. You are special. Vincent has a callin' to serve our country, and you have ta let others do what they're 'posed to do."

Tubby weighed his father's words. "He did say it's what he's 'posed to do," Tubby looked at his lap.

"Remember Tubby, passion is God's whisper that you are doing what ya came here to do," Myrtle interjected. "If this is Vincent's passion, then he *is* supposed to do it – just like you are supposed to watch over the animals. You wouldn't want Vincent to be mad at you for that would you?"

Tubby shook his head and reluctantly acknowledged that his mother was right. "I just feel bad for Mush," he sighed.

"You don't have to," C.J. patted Tubby on the shoulder. "There are lots of people who will be takin' care of Mush while Vincent is gone."

The next day, Tubby found Vincent first thing in the morning. "My dad said you's the bravest of the brave," he looked his friend in the eye.

Vincent smiled. "Tell him I said thanks. And Tubby, I love Mush and I will make sure that he is in good hands."

Tubby nodded and Vincent walked him to class.

Chapter Twelve

Tubby's head lay on Minnie's back. He felt her slow and shallow breathing lifting his head, then releasing it again. He had talked to Minnie long ago about dying. It was after Oscar had passed and he was heartbroken. He couldn't stand to sleep alone in his room without his best friend by his side. Much as he had been doing the past two days with his beloved pig, Tubby had gone to the barn and laid down next to Minnie.

"What's wrong Tubby," Minnie sat upright to look at the boy, who was by then a teenager of sixteen.

"It's too lonely in my room without Oscar," Tubby sighed. "I can't sleep without his snoring."

Minnie laid back down beside Tubby. She remained quiet for a moment, trying to find a way explain to him her beliefs on death. A few moments later she turned to him.

"Tubby, all of life is give and take. The sun will rise, but then it will set. If you just watch the world around you, you will see it all works like it was designed to. It's all perfect," she looked into Tubby's eyes.

"What do ya mean?" he returned her gaze.

"We are born in the spring. We grow and flourish in the summer. We begin to prepare for our transition in the fall and we finally sleep in the winter," she sweetly smiled.

Tubby frowned.

"No, don't be upset Tubby," she encouraged. *"Even when winter comes, there will always be a new spring to follow it. There will always be another birth and another cycle of life. This isn't the end for Oscar, Tubby."*

A tear slipped down Tubby's cheek.

"I knows it Minnie, 'cause all the other animals have said it, en they come back ta tell it, but I miss em. I can't think straight. I went ta gather eggs this morning en I found myself at the pond. I didn't knows how I got there or even whys I was there," he looked up at the barn ceiling, lost in thought.

"You went to the pond because that is where you would have gone with Oscar. And who's to say that Oscar wasn't there?" she asked him.

128

Tubby continued to stare above while trying to make sense of Minnie's answer. "Wadda ya mean?"

"Sometimes we are unaware of why we are pulled to certain places or toward certain things, but there is a reason," she paused to shift her weight and get a better look at Tubby.

"The spirits of those we love are trying to get us to remember the things we loved about them or the things we did with them. It's their way of trying to communicate with us – to let us know they are still with us. I bet the reason you ended up at the pond is because Oscar wanted you to go there to remember all the fun you both had together there. He wanted to let you know that he was still with you," she explained.

Although Tubby was accustomed to the animals knowing that life continued, he hadn't yet heard it enough by then, to trust it completely, especially since he hadn't seen it with his own eyes.

"I want ta believe that," he turned back to the pig, "but I's ain't sure. I wish I cud see Oscar again – just one last time."

"Tubby you know life doesn't end. It just changes its form. You don't know this but I have seen Oscar many times since he left. He is always with you, although you can't see him. If you just let yourself be still and quiet when you think of him. You will feel him."

Tubby raised himself to look at her again.

"Animals are different than humans," she explained. *"Our eyes have the ability to see the ones who have left. It's a gift given to us by God so that it won't be so hard on us here."*

Tubby knew on some level that Minnie spoke the truth. He couldn't explain why – he just knew. Still it didn't make it easier to prepare to say goodbye. Each and every animal he had ever known showed him unconditional love and respect. It wasn't like that with humans, sometimes, even with those who claimed to love him.

Losing his true friends was something he knew he would never get used to. He also knew that each time he lost another, the ache in his heart would grow a little larger. He wondered if at some point his heart would have no more room for anything other than its grief.

Tubby got off his stool and looked out the barn door. Beans and Charlie, were keeping a vigil. They looked at Tubby with forlorn eyes.

"How is she?" Beans asked Tubby.

"It won't be long now," he meekly answered.

Both Beans and Charlie lowered their heads as if in prayer. *"Tell her we love her,"* Charlie whispered.

"Yeah," Beans echoed.

"Why don't ya tell 'er yourselves? I think she'd be glad ta sees ya." Tubby opened the door to let them in.

"Hi Minnie," Charlie approached the pig. *"We just wanted to tell you goodbye."* Charlie's eyes gave away her sorrow.

Beans went to Minnie's head and kissed her there. Then he sat beside her.

"We're gonna miss you but I know we'll see you again. I just wanted you to know it though."

Minnie looked up at the two goats, a weak smile crossing her face. She heaved out a big sigh.

"I'm gonna miss you guys too."

"We'll let you get some sleep," Beans arose. *"Watch over us Minnie,"* he looked back at her.

"I will," she assured them, *"but you already have the best keeper you could have,"* she smiled at Tubby, who blushed a little.

"We know it," Charlie agreed, smiling at Tubby too. *"He sure is. Bye Minnie,"* she followed her paramour out the barn door, leaving Minnie and Tubby alone in the structure.

"You really are the best," Minnie looked up at Tubby. *"We are the luckiest animals alive to have you to watch over us."*

Tubby began to cry. "Yous ain't the lucky ones," he burrowed his head into the pig and choked back a sob. Then he wiped his face on the sleeve of his dirty shirt.

"I am."

Chapter Thirteen

The afternoon wore on, hot and sweltering inside the barn. It had been one of the hotter Septembers in Tubby's memory. He unclamped his overalls and slipped off his shirt before clamping them back. Minnie was sleeping peacefully and he debated on waking her to have her drink some water. He watched her labored breathing, and decided instead to let her continue to rest.

Tubby quietly tiptoed out of the barn to get a drink from the water hose outside. He stood, taking large gulps from the hose, while looking over the farm where he had spent all of his days.

There was nothing like it. Sure, it was small by most people's standards, but it had everything his family – and the animals – had ever needed. It was a perfect home.

Tubby surveyed the horizon. He saw Penelope in the north pasture, grazing. He remembered the conflict she had when C.J. had brought another milk cow home, a couple of summers before.

C.J. said he had run into some of the coffee gang at Stephen's Drug and they had asked him if he had any fresh milk to spare because, as a hobby, their wives had gotten into making their own butter.

C.J. had already been thinking about getting another cow after seeing an advertisement in the Konawa paper from a local ice cream vendor looking for ten or more gallons of milk per day. Between Penelope and the new cow, he could easily fulfill the order of the creamery and the coffee gang. It would also aid in bringing in some extra income for the family.

Things were falling into place for it to happen. C.J. just needed to sell the extra goats he had been saddled with. He could use the money from their sale to help pay for the new cow. It was a win-win situation.

C.J. also knew with Tubby about to graduate, he would have more time to help with the milking and deliveries. So, C.J. had gone to the weekly sale in Maiden, sold the extra goats and bought a young and very pretty Holstein cow.

"You can name her, son," he yelled to Tubby out his pickup window, as he backed up the trailer he had used to haul the cow home.

"Get 'er unloaded and take 'er on over and introduce her to Penelope. I bet they'll be the best of friends before it's all said and done," he added.

Tubby looked at the pretty black and white cow. He saw she was in turmoil and tried to comfort her.

"It's okay," he gently put his hand out asking permission to pet her. "I'm Tubby en I'll take really good care of ya," he assured.

"I don't want to be here. I want my old farm. I want my mom," Tubby heard her thoughts.

"I'm so sorry that you miss your mom," he continued to hold out his hand.

"You can hear me?" the startled cow backed up.

"Uh huh," Tubby nodded his head.

The cow looked Tubby up and down, and refused to speak until she had had time to comprehend what was happening.

"It's okay," Tubby repeated. "I promise I'll take great care of ya and you's gonna really like it here," he pointed around the farm.

The cow continued to watch Tubby without saying a word. Tubby didn't know what else to do to coax her out of the trailer, so he remained motionless, staring back at her until finally she spoke.

"I'm Miss Divine," she shyly uttered. *"My momma said I was the most divine bovine she had ever seen so that's what she called me – Miss Divine."*

Miss Divine began to leave the trailer, slightly pushing Tubby aside. When she got out, she looked around.

"That there is JoJo," Tubby pointed to the small coral where the horse was already examining the newest resident.

"Them chickens will have ta introduce themselves," he flatly stated. "I name 'em one thing en they goes en changes it, so I never knows who's who. 'Cept that one," he pointed to the rooster. That's Reddy. He's the boss of 'em all."

Ms. Divine ventured further away from the trailer and looked toward the pig pen.

"That's Minnie," Tubby pointed to the sow. "She's in retirement," he proudly smiled, remembering how he got his father to stop breeding her. "The other pig is Sam," he nodded to a black and white boar. "He's pretty new here too."

Ms. Divine continued the inspection of her new home. She nodded to the goats.

"That there's Pearl," Tubby pointed to the oldest goat, "en that un is Beans, en that un is Charlie, but she's a girl, not a boy," Tubby informed. "That un's Turner," he pointed to a wether. "En that kid is Sissy," he pointed to a bobbing white baby who was dodging her own shadow. "There's a few more of 'em out behind the barn. You kin meet 'em later."

Finally Miss Divine spotted Penelope in the North pasture, exactly where she was on that day.

"Who's that," Miss Divine motioned to the brown, cream, and somewhat plain looking cow.

"That's Penelope," Tubby smiled. "Yous girls will be the best a friends," he repeated his father's prophecy.

However, the prophecy didn't look as if it would come to pass. Penelope turned and saw the new milk cow and let out an angry and urgent "moo."

"Uh oh," Tubby turned to the newest addition to the farm. "Ya stay here," he told Miss Divine. "Let me talk ta 'er before ya meet 'er."

Tubby headed toward the pasture, looking back from time to time to make sure the new cow was obeying his request.

"Who is that?!" Penelope demanded as soon as Tubby was in ear shot. *"Why is that, that, that – thing,"* she finally managed, *"here?"*

"It's okay, Penelope," Tubby tried to soothe the obviously cranky heifer. "Her name is Miss Divine en Pa gots her so's he cud sell summa our milk en make a little more money."

Penelope was having none of it. *"I make plenty of milk. There isn't one thing wrong with the milk I make,"* she defended.

"I knows," Tubby agreed. "Ya makes the best milk ever! I loves your milk Penelope. It's just that Pa had some men asking if he cud git 'em some fresh milk for their wives en ya only make enough for us en the Fifes," he reasoned.

"Well I'll be," Penelope snorted. *"all you had to do was ask me and I'd been happy to make you more,"* she scolded, knowing she really couldn't have, but still wanting to save face.

"It ain't fair ta make ya do all that extra work," Tubby tried to get back in Penelope's good graces. "Ya already works too hard." He petted her head.

Penelope turned away from Tubby. *"I hope you don't expect me to share my stall with her,"* she sneered. *"I won't do it."*

"I'll tell Pa," Tubby acquiesced.

Tubby watched as Penelope lumbered away, mumbling harshly.

"Think they're gonna replace me with some little scrawny bovine," she sulked. *"Miss Divine my rump,"* she huffed. *"Miss Take is more like it!"*

Tubby giggled under his breath so as not to offend the already offended cow. *"Mistake,"* he replayed the angry cow's pronouncement, *"that was a good one if I do say so myself."*

Tubby turned back and made his way toward the new cow. He spent the walk trying to find a way to spin Penelope's instant dislike of her.

"Penelope wants ta stay in the pasture en eat some more," he tried to avoid the cow's gaze, knowing his face would give away the lie he had told.

It seemed as if Miss Divine was clueless as to what had just unfolded and she asked Tubby if she could rest.

"It was very hard to keep my balance in the trailer," she explained. *"My legs are tired."*

Tubby took the cow to the barn and put her in a stall next to Penelope's. Some of the goats were staying there, but Tubby decided to move them to the other side. He had a feeling that if Penelope would just take the time to get to know Miss Divine, they would indeed build a friendship.

"Everyone's got sumpin' in common," he thought to himself. *"As soon as they figure it out, they'll see they ain't that different."*

"Ya rest up. I knows ya had a hard day. I'll bring ya some fresh hay en some water in a minute," he told her.

"Tubby?" Miss Divine hesitated, still unsure that he could really hear her.

"Yeah?" Tubby whirled around to face her.

The cow took a step back, still in awe that he could.

"I'm glad you can hear me," she smiled.

"Me too. Be back in a bit," he returned the smile.

Chapter Fourteen

Tubby shut off the water, dropped the hose, and stood up surveying the pasture. Miss Divine was about fifty yards downhill of Penelope. He saw her turn back to the older cow and "moo."

"What're those two yammerin' bout now?" he wondered to himself.

The prophecy of friendship eventually turned into reality. It happened just as Tubby thought it would – through the two finding common ground.

When Penelope had finally decided to come in for the evening, she reluctantly took her place inside the stall adjacent to Miss Divine. Tubby had been in the barn, making sure all the goats were in and the chickens were cooped. Penelope let him have it.

"Why'd you put her right next to me?" she whispered to Tubby. *"We got a whole barn here and you could have put her down there,"* she motioned to the far end of the building.

"We're gonna be milking ya both. It don't make no sense ta have ya so far apart," Tubby tried to appease the ill-tempered beast.

Penelope hmphed her disapproval. Tubby heard Miss Divine try to introduce herself to her ornery neighbor, but with no success.

"Hi," Miss Divine, shyly nodded to Penelope. *"I'm Miss Divine."*

Penelope turned away and coolly ignored her. Miss Divine looked at Tubby who shrugged, not knowing what to say to the dissed cow.

Miss Divine sighed, then looked around the rest of the barn, introducing herself to some of the goats she hadn't met earlier. Tubby left for the night.

The following morning, Tubby went to milk Penelope first.

"Hi Penelope," he happily greeted her. "How are ya this morning?" he placed the milking stool below her stomach and sat down.

"Well actually," she snorted, *"I am extremely tired."*

"Really?" Tubby asked, a little startled. "Coyotes weren't trying to git inta the chicken coop were they?"

"No, nothing that simple," Penelope rolled her eyes. *"This one,"* she nodded her head toward Miss Divine's stall, *"decided that she was going to wail all night."*

Tubby looked around Penelope's big butt toward Miss Divine. Her head hung low in both fatigue and sorrow.

Tubby didn't know what to say to her that wouldn't offend the jealous Penelope, so he remained in silence the rest of the time he milked her.

When he finished with Penelope, he got new buckets and went into Miss Divine's stall. "How are ya?" he tried to comfort her.

"I didn't mean to cry," she whispered to Tubby. *"It's just that I miss my mom and my friends,"* she began to quietly weep again.

"I'm really sorry," Tubby apologized, as he stroked her nose. "I knows it can't be easy. I knows I'm not gonna like it when my friend Vincent has ta leave ta play army men," he bowed his head. "It's gonna be hard, so I knows how ya feel."

Miss Divine, nodded her head and tried to put on a brave face. Tubby looked over at Penelope, who's face had changed and seemed to be a little sympathetic.

Tubby, realizing that the sympathy might be a key to commonality between the two cows, questioned Miss Divine loudly enough that Penelope could hear.

"Tell me about your mom," he asked.

Miss Divine immediately perked up. *"My mom,"* she gushed, *"my mom is so beautiful. She's black and white like me and she has the prettiest brown eyes you've ever seen. She's so sweet too,"* she wistfully sighed.

Penelope had turned her head toward Miss Divine's stall so as not to miss the conversation. She leaned a little closer when Tubby told Miss Divine to continue.

"She told me not to be afraid when I had to go to the sale," the little cow remembered. *"She said everything was going to be okay. She said I'd be going to another farm to be their milk cow, just like she was the milk cow at my old home."*

"She was right!" Tubby smiled at the cow. "You's gonna be our milk cow, en Penelope kin help ya. Penelope's the best milk cow ever." Tubby sneakily looked out of the corner of his eye to make sure Penelope was listening to his praise.

"I would like that," Miss Divine lowered her head, not knowing if she was still going to be rejected by the older cow.

Penelope began to inch closer to the duo.

144

"I've never had ta leave my momma," Tubby continued his manipulations. "I don't know what I'd do."

"Well I had to," Penelope broke her silence as she sauntered the rest of the way to the partition between the two stalls. *"It was terrible. I remember it like it was yesterday."*

Tubby and Miss Divine turned to look at Penelope.

"I cried all night too, just like you did last night," Penelope confessed. *"I'm sorry, I didn't know that was why you were crying. I don't want you to worry though, Tubby's right. You really are going to like it here. We have great pastures to eat in and Tubby keeps the barn warm for us in the winter. Plus the rest of the animals are just lovely,"* she smiled. *"Well, except Reddy,"* she corrected herself. *"Reddy can be a mean ole rooster when he wants to be, can't he Tubby?"*

"Yep," Tubby agreed. "When I was little, he used ta chase me en peck my legs. One day he trapped me in Pa's truck bed en wouldn't let me out. Momma heard me hollerin' en she chased Reddy away with a broom." He chuckled, remembering the incident.

"Anyway," Penelope continued, *"you won't ever forget your momma, but the hurt will ease up. Especially when you make new friends here,"* she smiled. *"I'll take you out when*

Tubby gets through milking you and give you proper introductions."

Tubby smiled to himself. It was true, almost any conflict could be defeated when commonality was found.

Tubby stared out at the two cows, who had moved closer to one another. He could hear Miss Divine laughing hysterically at something that Penelope had said. As C.J. had predicted, after that first day the two cows had become the best of friends. Later Penelope had confessed to Tubby that she hadn't realized how lonely she had been for cow companionship until Miss Divine had come along.

"She gets me," Penelope had bubbled. *"She really is divine."*

Chapter Fifteen

Tubby returned to the barn with a tub full of fresh water for Minnie. He woke her and asked her if she would take a drink. She agreed and took a few sips before returning her head to the hay.

"Is there anything I kin git ya?" Tubby got down next to her and again, kissed her snout.

"No," Minnie answered. *"Just stay with me okay?"*

Tubby nodded his head. "I'm not goin' anywheres Minnie. Ima stayin' right here."

Tubby had not had that luxury with Oscar. He wished like everything that he had been given the opportunity to tell his beloved confidant goodbye, but it wasn't to be.

Tubby had been at school that early May day. The sky had looked ominous and foreboding for most of the afternoon. Tubby had wondered if Oscar would be scared.

With time's passing, Tubby's terror of storms had subsided a little, but Oscar still carried the scars of the day that the tornado took their house and split open Tubby's arm. He would often cower under the bed or get in Tubby's closet when he heard the rolling thunder making its way over the southwest hillside.

Tubby figured that Oscar wouldn't be at the bus to greet him when he got off. He was right. Tubby walked down the long driveway by himself, dodging large rain pellets as they tried to penetrate his clothing.

When he got home, he found his mother at the dining table sobbing. Tubby rushed to her.

"Momma, what's wrong?"

The sorrow on Tubby's face at seeing his mother cry, made her cry harder. She never wanted her boy to hurt and had always tried to shield him from everything bad in the world. On this day however, she knew there would be no protecting him.

"Oh Tubby," she rose and grabbed him. She pulled him almost through her, as if doing so would cloak him from what was to come.

"What Momma?" Tubby looked around frantically for C.J. "Is Pa okay? Momma, Is Pa okay?" He pleaded with his mother to respond.

Myrtle nodded her head, revealing that her husband was fine. "It's not Pa," she sobbed into an already soaked tissue. "It's Oscar," she whispered, lowering her head to look at the floor.

Tubby blankly stared at his mother, not comprehending that anything could ever be wrong with Oscar.

"He's probably under my bed Ma," he speculated, "or in the closet. Did ya look in my closet?"

Myrtle shook her head, "No Tubby, he's not in the closet or under your bed. He went out a while ago to wait for your bus. Mr. Martin, brought him back half an hour ago," she sobbed again.

"Well where is he and why did Mr. Martin bring him back?"

"Tubby, apparently Oscar darted out in front of Mr. Martin's pickup and he tried everything he could to avoid him, but he just couldn't."

Myrtle took her boy's face into her hands.

"He hit him and killed him." Myrtle searched Tubby's eyes for understanding.

Tubby shook his head no. "That can't be. Oscar never runs out in front of cars – ever. It wasn't Oscar Momma. It musta been another dog," he reasoned.

"Honey," Myrtle began to explain, "there was a really loud clap of thunder and lightning right before it happened. Mr. Martin thinks it scared Oscar and he bolted. I think that is probably what happened too. The lightning hit real close by Tubby. I even jumped when it happened 'cause it was so loud."

Tubby continued to stare at his mother, unable to believe that his best friend was gone.

Myrtle watched Tubby's eyes glaze over as the realization finally set it.

"Where is he?" he softly managed.

"I had Mr. Martin take him to the barn," she sniffed. "Tubby, I'm so very, very sorry."

Myrtle watched her boy-man lumber away, unsteady on his feet until he reached the door to the barn. He leaned up against it for a moment, trying to hold himself up. He stood there for what seemed like hours, but was really just moments.

He finally pulled open the big red door and went inside. Myrtle opened the back door of the trailer and stepped out onto the porch. A few seconds later, she heard the heart-wrenching wail of her son and she doubled over in her own pain, knowing there was nothing she could do to help him.

Inside the barn, Tubby saw Oscar lying on the straw near the first stall. He looked as if he were only sleeping. When Tubby got closer, he could see blood caked around Oscar's mouth and the side of his ear. He hit his knees, and not even realizing it, he let out a primitive and guttural cry. He sat down beside the dog and pulled him onto his lap. He stroked Oscar's head and sobbed, tears falling onto the dog's face, making it appear as if he too were crying.

"Oscar, I wished ya wudn't a come ta meet me. I wish yud'da stayed under my bed. Why didn't ya stay under my bed?" he pleaded to the empty body. "I wudn't a cared that ya weren't there. I wudn't a been upset. I'm so sorry I wasn't with ya. I'm so sorry I didn't get to tell ya goodbye."

With the word goodbye, Tubby unleased another wail. He sobbed while rocking his beloved dog back and forth until he collapsed onto his side, curled into a fetal position and lay there motionless for some time.

Minnie came and sat beside Tubby. JoJo came inside and stood over them both.

Minnie had played over in her mind how she could comfort the boy, but she finally realized there was no way.

"Tubby, we're all so sorry," was all she could think to say.

"Oscar was the best dog ever," JoJo added.

Tubby looked up at them and nodded his head in agreement.

"I didn't git ta tell em that," he broke down again. "I didn't git ta tell em how much I loved em. I didn't get ta say goodbye," he sobbed.

"Tubby, you told him that all the time," Minnie rationalized. *"Every day I heard you tell him how much you loved him,"* she reminded him.

"And I heard you tell him he was the best dog ever a million times," JoJo interjected.

Tubby nodded. "I knows, but I didn't git ta tell him one last time," tears continued to stream down Tubby's cheeks. "I just..." Tubby couldn't get enough air into his lungs to finish his sentence. He gulped from the lack of oxygen, trying to force it down his throat. His body shook and heaved as he tried to bring it relief.

"I just wanted…" he stopped again, "…I just wanted ta tell him one last time – just one last time," he whispered.

Minnie hung her head, wanting more than anything to be able to comfort her friend. She looked up at JoJo who returned her stare, his eyes telling her he also, had no answers.

"Oscar knows it Tubby," Minnie tried once again. *"He knows how much you love him and he knows you think he was the best dog ever. He knows Tubby. I promise you."* Minnie nuzzled into him. *"He knows,"* she delicately consoled.

Tubby fell into the pig and continued to sob.

"Shhh now," she whispered. *"It's going to all be okay,"* she worked him closer to her and let him cry.

Tubby eventually fell asleep against her and she gently laid down, so as not to wake him.

The two lay motionless for an hour before C.J. came into the barn. He looked at his tender-hearted son and a tear slipped down his own cheek. He didn't know how Tubby would manage to go on without his beloved dog. He knew he would, he just didn't know how.

Chapter Sixteen

Tubby had never been able to fully let go of the loss of Oscar. He still expected to see him in his bed when he awoke each morning. Instead, he was greeted by a cold and empty spot. When he looked at the barren covers, the old familiar pang of sadness would take a stab at his heart.

He could almost get through half a day without thinking about the dog, but invariably he would see something around the farm that would remind him of Oscar and it would send him deep into the memories of the moments they shared throughout their lives. As before, the piercing pang, like an ornery bee's sting, would engulf him, bringing with it a cascade of sorrow.

Tubby watched his Minnie and wondered if it would be that way when she was gone. He didn't know if he could take it. Just because he knew the animals' spirits continued, it didn't make it easier – especially when he wasn't able to see them himself. The nagging doubt of it all, scratched at the corners of his mind.

"Tubby?" he heard JoJo behind him and turned to face the horse. *"Anything I can do?"* he solemnly asked.

Tubby weakly smiled at his large friend. "You's really sumpin' JoJo. Thanks for askin' but I don't think so." He looked down at Minnie to make sure. She was still sleeping.

"I just wanna do something," JoJo looked at the dirt on the barn floor. *"I feel helpless. I wish there was some way I could help."*

"I knows," Tubby answered him. "But the best ya kin do, is pray for 'er."

"I been doing that," JoJo acknowledged.

"It's the greatest gift you kin give anyone," Tubby repeated the lesson he had once learned from the horse himself.

Back in grade school, one of his classmates, Tim Daniels, had died from meningitis. Tubby came home and moped for a couple of days until JoJo asked him what was wrong.

"Tim died en I don't know what ta do. His momma was at the school today gettin' the things in his locker. She cried en I wanted ta help her, but I didn't know how. I felt worthless," Tubby kicked the dirt.

JoJo nodded his understanding.

"There are times like that when we want badly to help others, but we can't find a way," he acknowledged. *"There are just some things we can't fix Tubby. But..."* JoJo looked Tubby in the eye, *"there is always one way to help."*

"How?" Tubby asked.

"You can ask the Maker to take care of them and give them peace. Ask Him to give peace to the family too."

Tubby blankly stared at the horse.

"You guys call it praying," JoJo stated. *"Animals just call it talking."*

"Animals pray?" Tubby raised his eyebrows.

"Well, it's not like we set aside a time do it, like when you go to church or at night before we go to sleep," he explained. *"We talk to the Creator all the time. We talk to everyone that watch over us,"* JoJo stated, as a matter of fact.

"Really?"

"Sure. They want us to talk to them. They like when we ask for their help. God likes it too. And face it Tubby; you, me

– all of us here – are really limited as to what we can do, but God and the angels aren't. They can do anything. So when you can't help someone, the greatest gift you can give them is to pray for them. You are bringing them the best help possible when you do."

Tubby stood a moment, contemplating what JoJo had imparted.

"That makes a lot a sense, JoJo. I knows I can't make Mrs. Daniels feel better, but they can," he pointed to the sky. "A lot better than I cud ever do."

JoJo smiled at the boy, happy that Tubby had been able to grasp what he had imparted. *"You go on now,"* JoJo motioned for him to leave. *"Go ask those who watch over us to help Mrs. Daniels."*

Tubby smiled at the wise animal and did as he was told.

Tubby watched JoJo leave the barn. He had become accustomed to "talking" to God more than praying, especially since he had suffered the loss of Oscar. Tubby figured it was because he used to talk to his constant companion, but found himself alone much more of the time. So when he continually found himself talking to the air after forgetting that Oscar wasn't around, he turned the conversation to one with his

Maker and those conversations seemed to help him feel as if he weren't alone. It also seemed to him that during those conversations, he was given clear answers to some of the dilemmas he faced.

The answers didn't come as a big, booming, God-like voice. In fact, it was quite the contrary. They came as a still, small voice that Tubby felt lived inside him. Although Tubby couldn't put his finger on exactly what made the voice different from his own, he knew it was. It felt different from his own voice and it certainly had more wisdom. It was also soothing.

In the beginning Tubby would sometimes doubt the answers he received, but it didn't take long for him to see that, when he chose his own way over the one imparted to him, the results were less than desirable.

The trouble with Roscoe mating with Mr. Fife's goat was the result of Tubby ignoring the still, small voice. Tubby had been talking to God and his angels about Roscoe, telling them he wasn't sure that the billy would follow through on his promise to leave Mr. Fife's goats alone.

In fact, he had experienced a bad feeling for almost a week. Tubby heard the voice tell him he ought to keep Roscoe in the far pen – the one that was as tall as JoJo's coral and had a better latch than the regular goat pen. But, because Roscoe protested, Tubby ignored the voice.

Billy goats, or bucks as they are called, stink to the high heavens most of the time. They are the owners of powerful scent glands that are used in a somewhat disgusting mating ritual. Bucks like to spray themselves with their own urine to attract does. In the years when the Andersons already had enough goats, C.J. made Tubby separate Roscoe as soon as he began to reek, knowing he was sure to be courting soon.

On that occasion however, Tubby felt sorry for Roscoe. He complained that he didn't like being so far away from everything, and he said he was lonely. So Tubby let the other goats roam, and kept Roscoe in the regular pen which was only four feet high.

That evening, Roscoe jumped the fence and pulled his Don Juan moves on Mr. Fife's Isabell. When Mr. Fife informed C.J. and Tubby of the impending birth, and Tubby subsequently questioned Roscoe, he realized that he should have listened to the voice instead of thinking he knew best.

After that incident, and a few others, ignoring the voice became harder to do and Tubby finally realized – beyond a shadow of a doubt – that his own ideas about things needed to take a backseat. He had learned that the small voice was never wrong. Never.

Tubby returned his gaze to Minnie. She began to stir a little, stretching her front legs and groaning. He leaned close to her and whispered into her ear.

"Wadda ya need Minnie? I'll get ya anything at all."

Minnie opened her eyes and with a frail smile on her face, looked up at the gentle giant.

"It's okay Tubby," she sleepily blinked. *"I don't need anything except you."*

"Ima gonna stay right here Minnie," he reassured her.

The two sat quietly for a few moments, Tubby, stroking Minnie's back.

"Hey, ya want me to tell ya what's been happening around the farm lately?" Tubby sat upright, thinking Minnie would be excited hear the newest events.

"I'd like that a lot," Minnie weakly smiled again.

"Well Delbert went all the way down ta the river en found a slew of snails. He ate every single one a 'em en he cud barely get his rump back up the hill."

When Tubby related the tale of his most cantankerous duck. Minnie chuckled.

"Henrietta has been hiding summa 'er eggs en we got three new chicks. Pa cudn't believe she was smart enough ta do that, but I knews it. Henrietta is one smart chicken," Tubby nodded to the pig.

Minnie's contentment at the unfolding dramas of the farm shown on her face and Tubby took it as a sign to keep going.

"Murphy found a scorpion en JoJo yelled at em ta leave it alone, but he didn't listen," Tubby sighed, remembering the cat's encounter with the arachnid.

"His paw is all swollen en he's limpin'," Tubby frowned. "Bet he listens ta JoJo next time," he added. "Oh, Fanny en Pooter knocked over Pa's Sheep Shower wine jugs en drank it. Them goats cudn't even walk straight," Tubby laughed out loud. "Pa was so mad."

Tubby continued telling Minnie about the important and not so important happenings, until he heard the gentle sound of her snoring. He bit his lip as he watched her chest slowly rise and fall. He knew he was in for one of the worst nights of his life and told God and the angels that he sure needed them by his side. He heard the still, small voice, whisper, "I'm here."

Chapter Seventeen

The afternoon wore on and Tubby could see Minnie becoming weaker. He knew the time for her transition was drawing near. He perched himself back on the stool and looked around the hot and humid barn. Minnie hadn't excreted anything since two days prior, but he thought that maybe he should freshen her hay anyway. He got up and walked to the tall stacks of hay and pulled a bale. He drug it up to Minnie's stall.

He got the wheelbarrow and went inside Minnie's stall and picked up as much hay from around her as he could pile on. He wheeled it out to the outside pig pen and threw it over the fence and into the mud. He hoped it might soak up some of the excess water that remained from the rain they'd had earlier in the week. Then Tubby went back into the barn and did it again.

Minnie hadn't stirred the entire time Tubby was working. He finally pulled the bale into the stall and cut the wires that held it together. He began to pull the hay apart and laid it beside her. He stopped mid-movement and realized it would be the last time he would do it for her. Hot tears began to slip down his face.

He pulled hay and wept, until it was all in place. He took the wires and the wire cutters out of the stall and set them on C.J.'s work bench. Then he hit his knees, quietly sobbing, so as not to wake Minnie. He didn't want her to see him cry because he didn't want her to hurt any more than she already did.

"Ima grown man now," he reminded himself. *"I have ta be strong – especially for Minnie."*

Buttercup, one of the nanny goats, nudged open the barn door and bleated at him.

"Shhh," Tubby put his finger to his lips. "Minnie's sleepin'." The goat nodded and backed out.

Tubby stood a moment longer at the workbench, trying to pull himself together. He heaved out a heavy sigh before returning to watch over his friend.

Tubby could see the light in the barn begin to fade. He got up and returned to C.J.'s work area to switch on the small light bulb that hung down naked from a cord attached at the roof. He heard Minnie stir and hurriedly ran back to her stall.

Minnie was trying to roll over, but didn't have the strength.

"Minnie, you wants me ta help ya?" Tubby asked.

She shook her head no. *"I don't think you can lift me Tubby. I'm fine right here,"* she accepted her locale.

Tubby sat down next to her and scratched behind her ear. "I loves ya Minnie," he kissed her head.

"I love you too Tubby," she replied.

"Do ya need any water?"

Minnie silently shook her head.

Tubby found it hard not to be able to help his pet. He wanted Minnie to need something – anything – so that he could be of help to her. Then he remembered to do the best thing he could do for her. He whispered to God and the angels to make her comfortable and to stay with her, bringing her peace. It had been the only thing that made him feel better all day. He wondered how muttering a few simple words could have so much power.

The light continued to fade and Tubby watched the shadows cast themselves upon the wall. He heard the chickens begin to file into the roost attached to the side of the barn.

"Minnie, I'll be back," he informed his pig. "I gots ta go lock up the chicken coop."

Minnie nodded.

As he walked to the coop, he remembered burying Reddy a year before after he had opened the coop one morning to find him dead. He never knew why, as the hens awoke at the same as he had discovered the lifeless body. However, Reddy had lived a very long life for a rooster, so he believed it must have just been old age. The thought gave him comfort.

The following day, C.J. had brought home a new Rooster named Rodney. He had bought the bird from Mr. Fife and the cock had fit in well with the rest of the feathered group.

Tubby walked into the coop. He told all the hens, the new babies, and Rodney, goodnight. They asked about Minnie.

"She's getting ready ta leave," Tubby choked back a sob. The fowl looked down in sorrow.

"Tell her goodbye for us," Henrietta said.

Bootsy, Pim, Retta, Sary, Mary, and Martha all echoed Henrietta's sentiments.

"Tell her she'll be missed," Rodney added.

"I will," Tubby agreed. "Goodnight everyone," he said as he closed the coop door.

Tubby returned to Minnie's stall and found her asleep. Darkness enveloped the barn, the small bulb at the workbench, the only illumination. Tubby sat on the hay and sighed. His mind and heart were fighting a terrible battle. His mind wanted Minnie's suffering to end, but his heart wanted more than anything to have her stay.

Chapter Eighteen

Suppertime came and again, Myrtle brought Tubby's food to the barn. She went into the pen and patted Minnie's head.

"I'm sorry Minnie," she said. "Thank you for being such a good pig."

A few minutes later, C.J. came in too and paid his respect.

"Thank you Minnie. Thank you for everything," he scratched her ear.

Minnie nodded.

"Pa, will you bring JoJo inside so he kin see Minnie?" Tubby asked.

C.J. obliged and JoJo walked over to the pen. He put his head over the top rail. *"I'm going to miss you Minnie,"* he said. *"You save a nice spot over there for me, okay?"*

Minnie nodded. JoJo left the barn, head low.

Much as he had done at lunch, Tubby merely picked at his food. He sat the mostly uneaten meal aside, then he laid down again next to his beloved friend.

"Talk to me Tubby," Minnie smiled. *"Tell me something funny."*

Tubby thought for a moment before he decided to tell her about his trip into town that morning.

"Ma sent me for them odor-eaters for my feet," he relayed. "She says my feet stink but I don't think they's that bad, do yous?" he looked at his companion, who weakly smiled.

"I went ta the drugstore en there was that purty blond girl there. I think she might want ta be my girlfriend," he wished. "She said she had a boyfriend, but I don't care." Tubby shrugged. "I told her that I cud beat him up so that she would know how big en strong I am." Tubby pulled up his arm and showed off his muscle to Minnie.

"Ya knows I wouldn't beat anyone up; would I?" he asked her. Minnie adjusted her head to look at the boy she loved fiercely.

"I tolds 'er we cud go ta the movie en then – here comes the funny part Minnie," he prepared the pig, while snickering in memory of the event. "I didn't mean ta, but I farted!"

Tubby laughed so loudly he startled the chickens in the adjacent coop. They clucked their displeasure at being awoken.

Minnie managed a small laugh and told her friend to continue his story.

"It was a real loud un. It was so loud, she heard it across the store," Tubby bragged. "I knows she likes me though 'cause I didn't have enough money ta pay for them Odor Eaters en she let me take 'em anyway," he exhaled, dreamily thinking back to their encounter.

"And guess what?" he turned to look down at the pig, "She sprayed Lysol so things would smell good for me!" Tubby could barely contain his excitement. Minnie snorted and adjusted herself, trying to get more comfortable.

"I knows she likes me," Tubby repeated, while smiling to himself. "That proves it."

"She would be lucky to have you Tubby. You are one of the best people I have ever known," Minnie blinked at him.

The two laid in the quiet of the barn, Tubby reliving his encounter with the woman of his dreams. Finally he spoke again but this time about his and Minnie's life together.

"Minnie, ya remember that time I tried ta ride your back en you took out underneath the Cedar trees en knocked me off with the branches?" Tubby laughed. "You is one smart pig," he petted her head. "I don't think I cudda thought ta do that."

"En you remember when Oscar got jealous a ya en rolled in the mud like you do? I guess he thought I liked ya 'cause you's always muddy."

Tubby sat up and swatted at a mosquito on his arm then he scratched it.

"Oscar thought if he got muddy too, I'd pay more 'tention ta him. He was a good dog wasn't he Minnie? Even though he was jealous of ya at first, he lernt ta love ya as much as I do. Remember when he would stay with ya all night while you birthed the piglets?" Tubby smiled down at his big friend.

Minnie rooted her snout under Tubby's hand, wanting him to stay close. They laid in silence for a long while before he lifted himself to look Minnie in the eye.

"Is ya afraid?" he hesitantly asked.

"No," the pig sighed. *"There's no reason to be."*

Minnie laid in silence for another moment and Tubby laid back down while he quietly stroked Minnie's snout and belly.

"I'm gonna miss ya. I don't want ta be here without ya. I'm going to miss ya like I miss Oscar," he sniffed.

"Remember when JoJo explained how we choose what we want to be before we come here?"

Tubby nodded.

"He's right. I chose this life and now, it is over. But only this life is ending Tubby. I'll have others and so will you. We'll even have others together," she comforted her friend.

"When ya leave, will ya be able ta see Oscar?" Tubby wondered.

"I can see him right now," Minnie answered. *"He's been here all day. He's going to help me cross. My mom is here too,"* a faint smile showed on her face.

Tubby laid back down.

"Will ya tell Oscar that I still love him?"

"He knows you love him Tubby. Remember when I told you he watches you every day. He will never stop loving you Tubby, and neither will I."

"So you's not afraid ta die?" Tubby asked again.

"I'm not," she answered. *"Dying is an illusion. It's as if we fall asleep in one room and awake in another. I may not be in the same room, but I still exist. You just can't see me because I'm in a different room. One day though, you'll come into the room too, and you will be able to see me."*

"When will I go ta that room?" he asked her.

"I don't know. But until you do, I will be able to watch you from my room. I will be able to see everything you do.

Sometimes you will think about me and you will wonder if I am seeing you. I want you to know I will be watching you right then, and I will give you a big hug. Close your eyes and be still. You will feel me. It may feel like the wind, but it is me."

Tubby nodded.

Minnie's breathing was becoming labored and Tubby wrapped himself around her in a hug.

"I love ya Minnie. I love ya so much. Thanks for being my friend. Thanks for all the fun we had together. Please hug me after ya leave. Please tell Oscar ta hug me. I love ya Minnie. I love ya," he cried.

"I love you too, Tubby. You are everything that was good about my life here. We will always be together because love never dies – ever. You be a good boy and you take care of the rest of the animals as good as you have taken care of me, because that is why you are here."

Minnie was struggling to get her thoughts out but she summoned all the energy she had left.

"JoJo told you that animals come here sometimes to help humans, but you came here to help us. You are the keeper of the animals, Tubby. You are our champion and you are very special."

Tubby stopped crying and sat up again. He instantly felt a knowing in the deepest recesses of his soul. It was true what Minnie said. It was true what Oscar had said. Taking care of animals was all he ever wanted.

In fact, as he looked back over his life with the animals, he could clearly see how he had made a difference.

He helped save Minnie from the heartache of losing her babies. He had helped JoJo when he had a lame foot. He had helped Oscar when he had been abandoned and left to starve. He had saved the baby chicks from the hawks and he had helped countless other animals in countless other ways.

"I'll take good care of 'em all Minnie," he sobbed. "I promise."

Tubby lay down again on Minnie and listened to her breathing begin to slow. He held her tight until she took a final heavy, heaving breath, and released it.

"I'll see you in the other room," Minnie whispered and smiled. Then she closed her eyes.

Chapter Nineteen

A few days had passed since Minnie's death. Tubby felt as if he was inside a thick, gray fog that he couldn't penetrate.

The first night, when he tried to sleep, he couldn't. He tossed and turned, finally giving up and watching the ceiling as if it was a television screen.

He and his father had buried Minnie up on the hill by the pond, where they had buried so many others. They laid Minnie to rest near the big Butterfly Bush, which had attracted masses of butterflies throughout the years. Tubby disclosed to C.J. that he thought Minnie would like that area the best, because she loved to watch the butterflies alight on the various wildflowers in the fields.

"She loved them butterflies. She once told me that they were her favorite thing 'cause they got ta change themselves from a caterpillar that had ta stay on the ground, ta a beautiful flower that cud fly."

C.J. had to agree with Minnie's assessment. "I always thought they was like flying flowers too," he smiled and patted Tubby on the shoulder.

"Minnie said that butterflies were a reminder that no matter where ya were – even if yous was at yous lowest – that God always had a way out for ya, en it was better than ya cud ever imagine," Tubby wistfully remembered.

"That Minnie was a smart pig," C.J. stopped his digging and looked at Tubby. "I've never thought of it that way, but she's right. Every time I've been in a jam and cudn't see my way outta it, things always turned out better than I cudda imagined it," he wiped his brow.

"She was smart 'bout a lot of things," Tubby replied. "She was the smartest pig I ever knowed."

The two men continued digging in front of the Butterfly Bush until they had a hole big enough to put Minnie inside. They then went to the barn and wrapped her in an old sheet. They tied the ends and attached it to the tractor before pulling her four-hundred pound body up the hill.

Tubby and C.J. pushed Minnie's body into its grave and began covering it with earth, while several of the chickens,

Rodney, the ducks, Penelope, Miss Divine, JoJo and the goats came to pay their respects.

"You wanna say something Pa?" Tubby asked C.J.

"Naw, you were her best friend Tubby; you should be the one to talk 'bout 'er," he answered.

Tubby looked at the animals surrounding her grave. He had to wait a moment before speaking. When he saw the sorrow on their faces, he realized it would cause him to choke on his own words.

He stood silent for a moment more while regaining his composure. Then he took a deep breath and smiled.

"Minnie was the best. She was so smart en she taught me so much. I've known 'er mosta my life en I never saw her unhappy. No matter what, she always found the good in everything."

JoJo nodded his agreement before Tubby continued.

"There was times I got mad over sumpin' en she would say to me 'Tubby, there's no reason ta git mad over that. Everything happens like it's 'posed to, just ya wait en see.'"

Tubby looked out over the crowd and smiled again.

"She was right ya know. It always worked out like it was 'posed ta. I loved 'er so much," he teared up and a little sob escaped him. "but I knows I'll see 'er again. We all will."

Tubby looked down at the earth beneath him. He took a deep breath.

"Bye for now, Minnie. Everything happens just like it's 'posed to."

Although it had been several days, sleep would not oblige Tubby. Finally, one night in the wee hours, he arose and walked to the barn. He entered Minnie's now empty stall and laid on the cold hay.

He looked at the ceiling for what seemed like a lifetime, trying to figure out how he could survive the all-encompassing grief that felt as though it would smother him alive.

He started and sat up when he heard someone behind him. Tubby turned around and right in front of him, there was Minnie.

She was more beautiful than he had ever seen her. Her entire being glowed with a magnificent golden-white light, as if she were illuminated from the inside out.

"Hi Tubby," she smiled at him, a smile so bright, and filled with so much love, it almost knocked him over.

"Minnie!" Tubby stood to his feet. "It's yous! It's really yous!" he squealed.

"It is me! I came back just to let you know that I'm okay. It's so beautiful here you can't even imagine it," she beamed. *"It's the most wonderful place I've ever seen. I can't begin to describe it."*

Tubby kept shaking his head, not believing what he was seeing. He finally got control of himself enough to respond to her.

"Minnie, you is so beautiful," he whispered. "Ya look like you's brand new."

"I am brand new," Minnie giggled. *"Everything here is brand new, no matter how old it really is. It's all perfect in every way. It's just like the caterpillar!"*

Tubby cocked his head wondering what Minnie meant.

"We are all just caterpillars when we are on Earth. When we die, we leave our bodies – our cocoons, and we turn into beautiful, perfect butterflies," she smiled again.

Tubby was again at a loss for words. He wondered if he was he imagining the whole thing. Was Minnie really there?

"I'm real," she answered him, even though he had not spoken his thoughts aloud. *"I can't stay, but I just wanted you to know that I'm so happy here and that we will see each other again. Until then, Oscar, Donald, Yeller Cat, Reddy, Pearl, I, and all the others, are watching over you always. You are*

never, ever alone Tubby," she blinked her beautiful blue eyes at her friend.

Tubby stood in awe, a tear slipped down his cheek.

"I'm so happy ta see ya. I wanted more than anything for yous ta come back."

"Tubby, I had to come back because there is something very important that I'm supposed to show you."

"What is it?" Tubby raised his eyebrows.

"You are doing what you came here to do Tubby and I want you to see what happens when souls follow their paths."

Minnie took her thoughts and projected into Tubby's mind the ripple effect that his love and caring for the animals had on the world.

"Look," she smiled.

What Minnie showed him was nothing short of a miracle. Tubby watched as a giant mass of energy – love – swept across the planet.

The mass was the love that poured from Tubby each and every time he gave of himself to his animals. All acts of concern and devotion cascaded out from him and coated everything it touched. They swept through the entire world like a gentle rain, cleansing negative energy, and changing it into beautiful, healing light.

Tubby witnessed the energy soothe a crying child, turning the baby's discomfort into coos.

He saw an arguing couple, stop, turn to one another, and embrace.

He saw a playground bully end an assault, and instead help the victim to his feet.

He saw those things, and a million other harmful actions, that were instantly transformed when the mass enveloped them. He couldn't believe that the incredible and astonishing changes he witnessed, happened all because he had loved and cared for the "least of these."

As Tubby continued to watch the events unfold, what he realized was, that just by loving, he had changed the world and made it a better place.

Minnie pulled back the images she had been showing him.

"You are doing what God entrusted to only you Tubby. Thank you for every way you made each of us feel special, and for every way you showed us we were loved."

Tubby stood in disbelief. He had never dreamed that doing what he loved more than anything in the world, could have the unimaginable effect it was having.

"You are so special Tubby," Minnie smiled. *"You are never to forget that, do you understand?"*

Tubby nodded his head, tears streaming down his face.

"I love you sweet Tubby. We all do – more than you can ever know. We will be here waiting for you when you are finished caring for the animals. Goodbye my precious boy."

Minnie disappeared and Tubby hit his knees, sobbing.

He looked around the now quiet barn. He looked to the goats, who were nestled in a pile, peacefully slumbering. He looked at JoJo in his stall, eyes closed, a smile settled across his dreaming face. He heard the chickens rustle a mere second before settling back into their cozy nests. He looked at Penelope and Miss Divine who were laying in their separate stalls, but each had a hoof touching the other. He saw the ducks, beaks tucked under their wings, as tranquil as the night air. Then he laid back upon the hay of Minnie's former stall and smiled.

"I'll never stop doing what I came to do," he told himself.

Then he fell fast and serenely asleep, blanketed by the spirits of those he loved, who had already shed their cocoons.

ACKNOWLEDGMENTS

During the darkest and hardest time of my life, an extraordinary soul came to be with me, who I believe was sent by God and my own angels. His name was Maxwell, and he was a beautiful, incredibly loving old soul, in the body of a dog. Maxwell was given to me by someone who has become a like a sister.

I knew from the moment I met Lynette LaMascus that we were kindred spirts. There was a knowing, deep in my soul, that she was an earthly guardian angel.

Lynette took care of Maxwell, after her cousin – who was Maxwell's first mom – passed from cancer. When I met Maxwell and Lynette, I too was battling my second diagnoses of breast cancer. From the moment I first saw the gray, fuzzy mop of a dog, I fell in love with him. I jokingly told Lynette that I would take him off her hands.

In her selflessness, she called a few days later and told me that if I was serious, she would let me take him. Maxwell was the greatest gift (next to my own children), that I have ever been given.

Maxi was so much more than just a dog. He instinctively knew I was in desperate need of his comfort because, along with the cancer, I was dealing with other catastrophic health issues, and I had just lost my father.

This amazing little soul stayed by side, comforting me, encouraging me, and helping me to find my own joy again. We got to spend almost eight magical years together, until he too, went to be reunited with his first mom in May of 2016.

To Lynette, who can never truly know the impact of her gift, I will be forever grateful.

To Maxwell, I thank you for allowing me to be your mom and for the unconditional love and support you gave me. I will never stop loving you.

To my lovely daughter, Elizabeth B. Wren, thank you so much for your work on the cover. You are incredible and amazing.

To my dear friend, Carol Cervi McCurdy, thank you for your willingness to read my stories and for your keen editing eye. You should rethink your career as a nurse and become a book editor instead.

And finally, to all of my friends, family, and readers, who continue to support this series, I am humbled and blessed by you. Thank you.

ABOUT THE AUTHOR

SD Shelton is the award-winning and best-selling author of the memoir *Me, the Crazy Woman, and Breast Cancer,* which chronicles her two diagnoses with breast cancer. She is also the author of *The Drugstore Series* and is a multi-award-winning former broadcast and print journalist. She loves everything Southern, including college football, the occasional evening cocktail, and sweet tea – gallons and gallons of sweet tea.

She resides in Oklahoma with her husband, Doug, and their three dogs, Teddy; and Walter and Harvey (who were born in her hometown of Konawa, Oklahoma, and have their own Facebook following under #BiteyBabies).

She loves to travel, play in the dirt, and roast her carcass on sandy beaches. Mostly, she loves to write.

Talking to Tubby is the third book of eight in *The Drugstore Series*. Watch for the fourth installment, about the town's "famous" actress, *Doll Dahl,* coming Fall of 2018.

Connect with SD on Facebook @SDSheltonBooks